SACRED SMOKES

D0366439

SACRED SMOKES

Theodore C. Van Alst Jr.

University of New Mexico Press — Albuquerque

Library of Congress Cataloging-in-Publication Data
Names: Van Alst, Theodore C., 1965– author.
Title: Sacred smokes: stories / Theodore C. Van Alst Jr.
Description: Albuquerque: University of New Mexico Press, 2018. | Identifiers:
    LCCN 2018008675 (print) | LCCN 2018011707 (e-book) | ISBN 9780826359919
    (e-book) | ISBN 9780826359902 (pbk.: alk. paper)
Subjects: LCSH: Indians—Fiction. | Gang members—Fiction. | Gangs—Fiction. |
    Street life—Fiction. | Short stories, American—21st century. | Chicago (Ill.)—
    Fiction.
Classification: LCC PS3622.A5567 (e-book) | LCC PS3622.A5567 A6 2018 (print) |
    DDC 813/.6—dc23
LC record available at https://lccn.loc.gov/2018008675

Versions of some of the stories included here
have appeared in the following publications:

Entropy: BlackCackle: "On Ice"
Noted: "Blood on the Tracks / No Mas"
Entropy: "Thunderbird"
The Raven Chronicles: "Bumblebee and the Cherokee Harelip"
Yellow Medicine Review: "Old Gold Couch"

Many thanks to all of you tireless and dedicated editors and staff.
The rest of you, support literary journals and magazines!

Cover illustration *Tobacco and Stars* by Lauren Monroe
Designed by Felicia Cedillos
Composed in ScalaOT 10.25/14

As always, for Amie, Emily, and Max

The Indian agent in 1854 wrote: "All bands of the Sioux have already received their presents with great appearance of friendship, excepting the Minnecow-zues (Miniconjou), Blackfeet (Sihasapa), and Honepapas (Hunkpapa). The former band are daily expected at the fort, and will gladly receive their annu-ities; but the Blackfeet and Honepapas still persist in refusing any annuities, and are constantly violating all the stipulations of the treaty.

"They are continually warring and committing depredations on whites and neighboring tribes, killing men and stealing horses. They even defy the Great White Father, the President, and declare their intention to murder indiscriminately all that come within their reach. They, of all Indians, are now the most dreaded on the Missouri."

—FRANK H. GILLE AND DONALD B. RICKY, *Indians of Oregon, Plateau, and Plains*

Contents

OLD GOLD COUCH

My dad smoked Old Golds. He became my pop because I watched a lot of *Sanford and Son* and, well, Redd Foxx is the shit, you know. I never told him why I called him Pop until he was much older. He was funny that way. Here's a good example of his low-key bigot stuff.

One day when I was about sixteen, Pop says to me,

What's the deal there, fiddy?

I'm like, Fiddy? What are you talking about?

He says, *Fiddy.* You always say

Fiddy dis.

Fiddy dat.

Gimme fiddy *cent.*

He's getting a li'l worked up now, says,

You dress like a Puerto Rican

and

you talk like you're black.

Shiiiiit, he finishes.

I don't know what possessed me (maybe the Mickey's Big Mouth Malt Liquor?) and I say,

We're going to have a discussion about stereotypes?

Do you know where we live?

I keep going. I say,

Look at you, man. We live in the middle of the city. You wear western shirts and cowboy boots every day. Do you think Dennis Weaver is going to step off some McCloud in downtown Chicago and offer you a job as an Indian extra on his show?

Ha ha ha, he says.

Shiiiiiit.

Like he always said.

And he never said a whole lot else, really. Shit. One time he didn't say a word for two whole weeks. What the fuck is that? Anyway, we had lived together since my ma kicked me out of the house when I was thirteen, a year or two after they got divorced. Said to go find the old man and live with him, see if he gave a shit if I kept a gun in the house, and a bunch of other crap that I tuned out, Ma sounding like the teachers on *Peanuts* and, after a couple of years, looking like them too. I searched all around the North Side of Chicago. Found him near Belmont and Broadway. We lived in a few different places on the North Side—roach motels, converted SROs, dumpy apartments, tiny studios. I was a teenage gangbanger, he was a middle-aged alcoholic, and we were Indians in the city, mostly unmoored and ignorant in more ways than I can count. We sort of had each other, knew each other even less. When I moved in, the old man gave me two rules and a gift:

1. Don't get busted, because I'm not coming to get you.
2. Never cheat on your girlfriend. If you're done, just end it. I never cheated on your mother.

Then he said,

Here's a map of Chicago,

and,

Don't get lost. I'll never find you.

I memorized that map. I can still visualize it, clear as day, and get to any part of the city I want. Along with that map, and the moving out of my old neighborhood and going to school halfway across the North Side, I became extremely familiar with every set, every gang, every branch of Latin Kings, Gaylords, Insane Deuces, Mexican Playboys, Spanish Cobras, Harrison Gents, Maniac Latin Disciples, Vice Lords, Black Gangster Disciples, Latin Eagles, Lovers, Counts, Hoods, and all the rest in the hundreds and thousands at least from Howard Street on the north to Division Street on the south, and from the lakefront on the east to about Kedzie on the west. I think it's around twenty-four square miles total. And I learned pretty quick how to draw all of their symbols and shit upside down and backwards.

Just so you know,

there are a *shit ton* of gangbangers in Chicago.

There's a *lot* of graffiti to learn

and

you better learn how to fight, if you don't like to run.

Anyways, my pop smoked Old Golds. A *lot* of Old Golds. You have *no* idea.

On weekends sometimes, if we both happened to be home, he would say,

Hey. Let's count.

Shit.

We would have to count the fucking coupons that came with each pack of Old Golds. He saved them all. But this wasn't the Camel / Marlboro Miles foolishness that could get you a belt buckle or a pool table or whatever. You could buy shit with the Old Gold coupons.

His dad smoked Bel-Airs, and those had coupons too. I don't

remember *him* counting any coupons, or getting us to do it, but Grandpa never seemed to be interested in the coupons except as something he got out of the tobacco company. What he was *really* interested in was the little gold peely things that came off when you opened up a pack of smokes. He would burn them—well, not burn them, but he would sort of melt them. He would sit at the kitchen table with his big, weird ashtrays and he would trace his lit cigarette about a sixteenth of an inch along the gold strands. They would twist and curve depending on his movements. He was like the director of a flea circus or something, with these little curly twists of gold arcing and folding in his orange plastic arena. And the best part was that he wasn't limited to his tiny pastime by the opening of a pack of cigarettes, though that seemed to be a fairly frequent occasion, because he smoked a *lot*. Nope. He had a pile of the friggin' things. Folks would save them and bring them to him. All he had to do was reach behind that dusty bottle of Pinch that looked like a big butterscotch candy on the little shelf that ran under the kitchen window and take out another whenever he felt like it.

My dad burned those things too. I did as well, of course, but the skills of grandpas tend to get lost in successive generations.

Pop burned different things with great success.

He also liked to light stuff on fire. He would burn pine needles in his outdoor ashtray when he got older and moved back to Michigan, into Grandma and Grandpa's house after they passed. But when we lived together in the apartment he would burn coleus leaves in the ashtray. When you touch a dried coleus leaf with a lit cigarette, it smolders and burns in fits and starts like gunpowder.

Sometimes he would burn dandelion greens in the tub, but I never figured that one out.

We counted and counted and counted the coupons. They were green as fuck. But minty green. He smoked a *lot* of Old Golds, and he'd done so for a long time. How long? When he would buy them in the store he would ask for two packs of Old Gold Filters. That's how long. When I would forge the notes that you probably couldn't get away with nowadays they would say,

Please sell my son a package of Old Gold Filters.
Thanks,
Pop

The coupons.

If you go online you can find some of the old (Old Gold!) commercials and a picture of the coupons (5 Gift Stars!). In case you don't believe me (I played them for my wife and she says it even sounds like the old man): http://www.archive.org/details/tobacco_dpr91e00 here.

There you can be seduced by a guy who sounds like a cross between Claude Akins and Allen Baron's Baby Boy Frankie Bono from *Blast of Silence*, but if both were really high on syrup. He says, "Old Gold Filters. The cigarette for independent people. Old Gold Filters. A delicious mixture of rich tobacco flavors. Flavors that never came through a filter before."

5 Gift Stars!

That's right.

Coupon Saturday. We're counting away. Stacks and stacks of these friggin' coupons. With some rules. Each stack had to be yay high. Sold by weight, not by volume. Yay high. And when you were done, you put a little slip of paper on there with the amount of coupons and the amount of points. I think there were some Gold Gift Stars! that might have been worth something different, so you prolly would have to do some math, too.

You all want to know, don't you? How many fuckin' coupons, man?

A *lot.*

Like I said. *Stacks.*

One time the coupons bought us some dishes (and here is where things get foggy, or smoky, depending on your point of view).

Oh yeah. About the dishes. I told this story to one of my aunties over the phone a couple of months ago. I won't say she's my favorite, in case this ever gets printed. Man, she said. I never heard that one.

We had dishes. I'm not gonna lie to you and say we ate off of paper towels and whatnot, even though that would come later for a while. We started out with dishes anyways. The problem was, the problem with the dishes was, they had to get washed.

Hey, fiddy. You gonna wash those dishes?

Yup, I say.

When?

Today I guess.

You better.

Another day goes by.

Speedy. You gonna wash those dishes?

Speedy? you're sayin'. Where did that come from? When I was a little dude, I wasn't too enamored of the walking thing. So, I scooched on my ass wherever I went. And apparently I went everywhere. And I was *fast.* So why would I bother with some new method of perambulation? So fast, my old man nicknamed me Speedy. And it stuck. For a long time. But none of my friends ever called me that. Ever.

Yeah, Pop. I'll get 'em.

And this went on for a bit. But you have to know, Pop came home drunk. Every night. Usually about 10:30 or 11:00. And that was good. Because the restaurant next to the roach motel on Broadway near Buckingham with the Murphy bed that we used to live in would still be open.

He would open the door with his soury breath and say,

Jeet?

I'd say,

No. Jew?

He'd say,

Squeet.

And off we would go, down to the diner. Do you know what a Francheezie is? Look it up. But in my fourteen-year-old eyes it meant love. Or something like that.

One night his breath opened the door, but it was only 8:00.

Shit.

Thought you were going to do those dishes.

I forgot. I'll do 'em right now.

There's a whole fuckin' sink full of fuckin' dishes, goddamnit.

I'll get 'em.

A whole fuckin' sink full.

I'm gettin' em.

A whole fuckin'

goddamnsonofa

bitch!

Crash, he puts his fist through a sink *full* of dishes.

Again.

And again.

And again.

Blood and shit is everywhere.

Fuck, I think. I'm gonna get it.

He looks at me. And his eyes refocus.

And get smaller.

And he breathes out of his nose.

That's not good.

And he whips his drunken head around.

Don't wanna wash the fuckin' dishes?

he says in that falsely calm and controlled voice of the person thinking of unleashing even more.

Don't wanna wash the fuckin' dishes?

FUCK IT.

You don't have to.

And that motherfucker started pulling out dishes from the cupboard and breaking those in the sink too. Clean fuckin' dishes.

BAM. Coffee cups fly. Cheap but sharp-as-hell porcelain shards would be picked out of the insecticide-soaked carpet (tile? asphalt? the apartment was in a building that was a hotel back at the turn of the century but had been rented by various chronological contracts for many tired years) for a long time coming.

BAM. Plates smash. Loud enough to hurt.

BAM.

BAM.

BAM.

There. You won't have to worry about doing any fuckin' dishes at all.

Clean that up.

BAM

went the door.

Ho-lay. Aunt Jessie was laughing big tears when I told her that one, but I tell it to her a little different.

The other day I was txting my daughter back because she's away at school and wanted to know what Indian Summer is—she says there's a song that says something like, "UR an Indian Summer in Winter," so while I'm writing (I don't txtmebck well) and listening to Gordon Lightfoot tell stories from the Chippewa on down about the big lake they call Gitchigoomi I text her back and tell her about NDN Summer, and she texts back in about one fifth of the time and says,

Oh okay thats

been bugging me
forever
sorry had to ask
thanks ☺

Guess her ma's not in the kitchen breaking any dishes now is she?

But here's the deal with the dishes. I thought either we'd need to use some of the coupons to buy the dishes that were, uh, lost, and then find some dough to buy the couch that we were gonna need because my ma had just kicked my brother out too, or we'd be sleeping on the floor and eating off napkins, but that ended up not being the deal. This is what I remember.

We had a big coupon Saturday. A good one. One of those ones that after the counting we could go to the bar and I would eat caramel corn and drink nasty bar cokes and hear jokes about Six-Pack Annie until all three would make me sick. We busted out *all* the coupons, *all* the shoeboxes, *all* the coffee cans, and a secret stash of some other ones that I had never seen before.

Some big shit was about to go down.

Speedy. We're getting a couch.

What?

A couch. Clean the shit out of your ears.

How are we gonna get a couch?

With these.

The coupons?

I wanted to say,

With the motherfuckin' Gift Stars old man? Can those fuckin' things buy me some pants that fit?

Yeah. The coupons. Jesus Christ. Get your shoes on.

Where we goin'?

To get the couch. Jeee-eee-sus Christ. Smoke, smoke, smoke.

No, where are we gonna get a couch?

At the Nelson Brothers.

Shit, I thought. By the old neighborhood. That's at Broadway and Lawrence. Gaylords. Uptown Rebels. Assorted hillbillies. By the Sears where I got into a humbug with a punk-ass GL from Sunnyside and Magnolia. Pushed him into a rack of Dickies, and we beat on each other for a minute, and the old man was like,

What the fuck?

I told him,

I told you not to bring me here.

He goes,

It's a fucking Sears.

I'm like,

He's a hillbilly Gaylord. What do you expect?

Jeee-eee-sus Christ.

How are we gonna get a couch on the bus?

What?

They'll deliver it?

Yeah.

Should I get the coupons?

Bring 'em.

Now I say,

Jeee-eee-sus Christ.

And I smoke, smoke, smoke.

But I think,

This'll get rid of these fucking coupons once and for all.

So we got a couch.

And the color?

It was Old Gold when we got it new.

When I was a kid, I collected hockey, baseball, football, and basketball cards. And I wouldn't really look at them, but I would count them. And stack them. And rubber-band them. Stan Mikita. Tony Esposito. Lew Alcindor. Bobby Douglass. Mickey Mantle. Harmon Killebrew. Stacked and numbered. Banded and dusty.

Jeee-eee-sus Christ.

Thanks, Pop.

JAGG'D

Get me the fuck out of here, he says. Teeth and jaw clench, unclench.

Me and Freckles are looking at Gooch strapped in this contraption that looks like what they call now an elliptical machine but it's a bed that revolves around or whatever because Gooch is paralyzed and they have to rotate him or something. I don't know. What do I know? I'm a fuckin' kid.

Get me the fuck out of here, *now*, he says. Clench, unclench.

Gooch can't go nowhere without us, and he knows it. We know it too. That doesn't make it any less scary, but I'm starting to get the feeling we're gonna be stuck with him if we do this thing.

He's paralyzed. From the waist down. He got that way when some Harrison Gent put six bullets in his back, said fuck it, reloaded, and gave him one more for luck. His jaw broke when one of the bullets, maybe that last one, tore up through his shoulder and into his face. He's been this way for just a little while, but he's been in the hospital for way too long. I can see it in his face. Him and his brothers all kind of look the same, but different. Gooch is the oldest, and hanging there, looking down on us a little, from that big rotating bed, his face is drawn, but really alive. His hair hangs down kind of on the one side, but I can still see he's using Vitalis in it. I think him and his brothers have parents who must've rowed over on the very last cases of it in the world when they moved here from Ireland in the '50s. They all look like Greasers, and at least one of them actually was, from Howard Street. A couple of the others were TJOs, and Gooch here, he of the gaunt, and haunt, well, Gooch is a Satan's Disciple.

Freckles and me, we're not SψDs. Still though, we spin the bed around, the elliptical part, but not too fast. I tried. Was all,

Hey, Gooch,

wanna go for a ride?

He gives me the look,

that one that says,

I'll fuckin' kill you, Teddy,

but his mouth never even moves.

No clench, no unclench.

So we take it easy, get him spun around to where he's lying on his back.

Prop me up, fuckers. He starts the *wwwnnnnnnnnngngnggnn* motor thing and the bed raises up slow like, Gooch looking like a resurrection, I guess, I think. We're in a semi-private room in St. Francis. Seems like as good a place as any for a revivification.

Give me that bottle of Jack, he says. I know you brought it.

Freckles, that ginger ass-kissin' hillbilly double, gulps his too-pointy Adam's apple and almost fuckin' says,

Yessir.

Does this motherfucker have Vitalis in his hair too? I ask myself, looking at that greasy red mop (and this red hair ain't like Muck's, which we all know—because we always tell him—is red as the head of a dick on a dog). Have some self-respect for fuck's sake, I say.

What? Freckles says.

Nothin'.

Help me get this pillow behind him, I say.

Gooch is just chugging that Jack with the side of his mouth,

straining it through his teeth,

spilling just a little.

Goddamn, Gooch, I think,

but instead I say,

Hey, Gooch,

you want some pop with that?

Yeah, he says.

A coke or something.

Freckles, go get Gooch a coke or something, dipshit, I say.

Fuck you, Teddy. He stomps off down the hallway.

Gimme a smoke, Teddy, Gooch says. Clench, unclench.

I don't think we can smoke in here, I say.

Fuck that, Gooch says.

What are they gonna do? Take away my legs and strap me to a bed?

Clench, unclench.

What about your buddy over there, I say. Isn't that an oxygen tank?

So? Gooch says. Just don't smoke by it.

Hahaha. We laugh and light up some smokes.

Doesn't the nurse ever come by? I say.

Yeah. Sometimes, but not much. There's a couple of 'em that are okay, but the day shift one is a bitch, he says.

Clench, unclench, clench, unclench.

Hunh, I say, and flick my ashes in a plastic water cup.

Freckles comes back with a can of coke.

Here you go, Gooch, he says.

Get me some ice, bitch, Gooch goes, and gives me a wink as he hands the bucket to Freckles.

Freckles stomps back out and down the hallway again.

So what are we gonna do? I say.

Get me the fuck out of here, like I said before, he says.

Clench, unclench.

Shit, man, I think.

He was fuckin' serious.

What do you want me to do, man? Just put you in a chair? I say.

Yeah. Like that, he says. Just put me in a chair and wheel me the fuck out of here.

I clench, unclench.

I do this, because Wacker.

A couple of years ago, on my thirteenth birthday, Wacker got out of jail. I didn't know him then, had never met him. We were all hanging out at State Park (before the city took it over and made a golf course out of it—what the fuck?) and there were like these two KKK guys who were bugging me to paint a mural for them, pressing me, because I had some definite skills in the art department, could even write upside down just as fast as right side up and draw any gangbanger shit you wanted. Telling me they would take me here and there. I could draw, so, yeah. And Wacker, who had just been sitting there, being quiet and saying nothing, says,

Man, get the fuck out of here with that shit.

Nobody wants that shit around here,

fuckin' Klan shit.

Fuck you.

And these two redneck fuckers just backed away,

took off,

looked back,

and

Wacker made

this face

that made

them not look back again.

It wasn't exactly a reverse of that time the Choctaw took up a collection to help the Irish, but yeah, it was close enough, and the sentiment was the same.

Thanks, man. What did you do that for? I say.

Fuck those guys. Stupid-ass Klan.

Draw murals for us, he says.

Fuck them.

Forever.

Damn straight, I thought.

Yeah, I say.

Fuck them.

Somebody told me it's your birthday, Teddy, he says.

Yeah, I say. I guess so.

Shit. Well all right.

Open this, he says

and

hands me a brown paper bag with the coldest quart of Old Style I've ever had before or since. Shit. I can taste it right now. We had other shit to drink, wine and Mickey's and whatnot, but all I can remember really is that brown glass bottle full of beer, sweating in the bag.

Damn.

I chug a bunch and

hand it back to him.

We don't talk really. Or not much. Or actually, we talk like guys talk when they meet each other. We say what's up and hey not much and yeah. I think we think a lot, but we don't say what we think. We all look like we're making James Dean face, or Michael Beck from *The Warriors* face, or one-thousand-mile-stare face, any and all the faces not our own. Your face is the cover to your book.

And if you look out and off to the side from it, under the scratched-out title, well, no one can read that, can they?

How old are you, man? he says.

I say, Thirteen.

Hunh, he says. Well all right.

We finish the bottle.

Better get some more, he says.

Yup, I say.

We'll do whatever, I guess.

He's buying.

We walk around, check shit out. It's not too hot out—it's just starting to be summer in the city, still nice, especially in the early evening. That smog-inflected pinkish sunlight, and the nighthawks, and the cool breeze, the not-yet-hot winds that tell so much, full of food smells and little kids laughing up on third floors. That light. Not much is happening here. It's a park that's been kind of abandoned by the state. You have to hop a barbed-wire fence to even get in. It's overgrown and cool, with a big lightning-struck willow in the middle that sits over what we called a lagoon. I always think Saruman would totally hang out here and boss around hobbits. There must have been a spring to feed all that, because there was a little river attached, and you could Huck Finn that shit if you wanted. Me and Idiot tried it one time on this old, green-painted section of fence, but it didn't really work out. I started thinking how no one would come looking for us, and that made me say fuck it. I didn't want to give anyone the satisfaction of me being right.

We get bored after a bit and need something to do. I know this guy Marty who lives close by. I remembered some things about him that you could always count on: food in the house, a hot sister, a stepmom from Mexico who smoked much weed, and an out-of-town dad. Plus Richard Pryor, Redd Foxx, and Cheech & Chong albums. The first time I ever smoked weed was at Marty's house. He used the cardboard tube from a tampon and some tinfoil to make a pipe. I think that's where I learned you could just make shit you needed and that you didn't always have to have the store-bought crap.

We head over to Marty's. We're kind of drunk, and I'm thinking pickles or something. Marty's is the first place I had hot—like spicy hot—food. Hot homemade pickles. That are super hot when you're high. That would be alright.

We're almost there when we run into this dude. I can't remember his name—it's like Dave, or Rickey, or Carlo, or some shit—I don't know. Chunkychubby whitish guy.

What's up, we nod at him.

Nothin', he says.

Randall goes,

Hey, you still got that sweater?

Which one? he says.

He's got more than one? Wacker says.

Apparently, I say.

The Imperial Gangster party sweater, Randall goes.

Yeah, Dave or whatever his name is says.

Randall says, Well let's check it out, fucker, and then makes this weird cackly laugh like he would sometimes. He looked like Justin Timberlake. But he could, because his brothers all boxed Gold Gloves.

The sweaters he's talking about—I don't even know if they make them anymore, but back then those cardigan-style sweaters were the shit—they were everything. Those were your colors. Man. And not like that boring LA-style duo-color shit they would try to bring later on, that shit that we told them, yeah, we're all set with the whole club thing here in Chicago. We been gangbangin' for about a century or more here, so thanks anyway. Yeah, sure they were your colors and that meant the same and all, but our colors were *colors*. All the sets had two colors—most were black and another color (except for 6-Corner Hustlers—theirs were red and blue—ha—LA style). War sweaters were mainly black, and your secondary color would be at the cuffs, shoulders, lapel, and for chops (rings) around the arms. Green, grey, turquoise, orange, brown, white. You name it. Party sweaters were a reverse of that pattern, and in this case, this particular IGC sweater we were wanting to see was a mostly pink party sweater that Dave or whatever says he gangstered off someone on the West Side. My eyebrow goes up a little there looking at this guy when he says it, but whatever, sure.

He comes out of the hallway of his apartment building leading with the sweater. Man, that fuckin' thing is pink as hell. Not hot pink and black, but powder pink and black. Nice. Has a big old upside-down banana-yellow and black crown 👑 patch on the front and *Latin King Killer* embroidered across the main belt on the back. Crazy Gangster shit.

And I keep staring as Dave or whatever rolls up holding that IGC party sweater and *wearing* a Harrison Gents war sweater. This fuckin' guy. Yeah. HfG's colors are black and purple. Man—that is a nice-looking sweater. Dave or whatever has no idea that we were gonna gank that fuckin' IGC party sweater from him, but yo, this motherfucker has just added a bonus.

Dave or whatever, Wacker says. Are you a Gent? You ride HfG?
Yeah, Dave or whatever says.
Thought you were Chi-West, I say.
I used to be, he goes.
Wacker says, You a fuckin' club hopper, Dave or whatever?
Nah, man. Just, you know.
No. No I don't know, Wacker says. He don't know, he says, Teddy. Fuck, man, I think.

I know, I say.

Wacker looks at me and his eyes say, Yeah, I think I know too, and

he busts Dave or whatever clean in the mouth with a Mickey's green

hand grenade bottle and

I think, Well, that's gonna need some wiring and shit,

then everyone beats the ass off of Dave or whatever.

Randall takes the 𝕵👑𝕮 sweater and

Wacker gets that fine 𝕳 ʃ 𝕮 war sweater and

we all drink a bunch of Mickey's Big Mouths and

listen to Dave or whatever recover.

And

Wacker is Gooch's younger brother.

We drop acid. Gooch loves taking acid. He also loves drinking and smoking weed, and doing tic, and hitting the rag, and everything else he can think of that I think can take him out of this . . . chair. We drink for a while, waiting for this blotter to kick in, and then right when I feel the corners of my eyes tighten up and my face reach out into the universe, Gooch says,

Teddy. Tell us a story, man.

Yeah, Midget, tell us a story, someone behind me says. I don't see who it is because the whole back of my mind just turned purpley black, and tiny, pale-blue braided lightning pops behind my eyes. I say,

Sure.

This is what happened, I say.

This is what I tell them.

Cold ash drifted down, solemnly and slow, like the late autumn traces of a paper wasp party favor. From where he stood, he saw light seeping over the ridgeline, thin bars of yellow and orange that began to

light the faces of the men who muttered and turned things in the mud, the tilt of their heads and tone of their voices subtle tells that described their confusion.

Had it rained mud, rolled ball lightning, had hot air forced hotter air from his lungs, he would have been accepting of the situation and remembered more . . . interesting times. This, though, he could not abide.

He called for his dogs.

One by one, curs of all colors came silent over the spine of the ridge. Eyes dully glowed, muzzles nuzzled the blackened earth. Blues and brindles stopped and cut their ears toward whines unhearable by human cohabiters of the shattered woods.

With low moans that turned to quiet howls they moved like twists of carbon black through the flowing smoke, their eyes winking embers that flashed and faded. The men gave them an ever-wider berth.

The dogs nodded and paused among themselves. Heads lifted and dropped; paws turned and padded. Men muttered. The troop considered the growing pack. The soldiers were silent. No stray potshots erupted from the picket.

The light reddened, then began to blue.

How many were lost? asked woefully green Lieutenant S. L. Hubbard, a couple of months out of West Point.

Quite a few, said Sergeant Isaac Uncas Lonegan, a man whose braids were turning grey when this young artillery battery section officer was just learning to read.

Well then, let's get a burial detail, Sergeant Lonegan.

Sir, if I may, there's protocols, sir, what need to be followed here.

What need to be followed, sergeant, are my orders.

As you wish, sir.

The sergeant strolled out of Lieutenant Hubbard's tent and angled toward a mass of questioning men.

He had watched them curse and tug and wrestle the two cannons up and over the hillocks that would become this small range. Observed the day's and night's grinding routines that marked the dull progress of soldiers. Smelled the horseshit and the burnt moldy beans before and after they made their way through this outlying company. He wondered at their location, how and why they were so far from the nearest large encampment.

He wondered if they'd be missed.

The lieutenant wants us to form a burial party, boomed the sergeant.

The men laughed nervously and stamped their feet against the cold.

The sergeant reared his head back, cocked his scratched glass eye down at the troop, and bawled,

That would be now, yer royal highnesses! Let's get to it! an odd and hitching urgency in his bellowing.

No whines of, Sarge, we haven't been ta mess yet. No bullshit under-the-breath comments about him being an Indian. No hustling smokes. No name-calling, no grabassing, skylarking, horseplay, or shenanigans. All stern these boys were tonight. A work party for burial detail was serious business. When it was proper. It was an age-old duty, and an age-old honor. The duty NCO, Corporal Sprouse, called the squad to order, and off they went.

They tramped by Sergeant Lonegan, who was licking a pencil and composing what looked to be the very last letter from the earth, or at least the last one from him that would be delivered to his reservation back in Connecticut. He tapped a dirty finger on his prosthetic orb as he carved the shapes of words into the paper. His face worked hard as he squinted and sighed. Hut one hut two went the men going past.

Letters appear from soldiers never heard from again. Killed in action. Missing in action. Spirits make their way back to their loved ones, but the bodies don't come home. Chapters for those families don't close, and the wounds throb and linger, worse sometimes during storms, when the flash of blue and the whine of white in the sky send the mind far off, reeling in places where we picture the thrumming rains washing the mud from the faces of long-buried loved ones, those untended, those who gave all.

Bleached and picked-clean bone reaches into our warmed family spaces, says its peace—remember us—and returns to its churning resting place, never quiet, marker of maddened souls who forever follow camps of men who fight and bleed and die, in the end none of them ever quite sure why.

From high in the swollen sky a purple thunderbolt arced down to split an old, greying willow. He walked through the smoldering leaves and the blackened heart of the now-dead tree. Owls called from the thick damp of the tree line, wet cotton hung from branches of beech and buttonwood, hickory and chestnut. Frogs carried on about their business, and crickets ran out of their way while cicadas wound down for the evening. Vermin and detritus skittered behind him through the dry, dead leaves. He trailed his long, thin fingers along the trunks of the sugar maples as he walked, leaving oozing, sap-filled scars that chrysopoeiacally filtered the dying light of day. The dogs, now gathering on the hillside, shuddered and whined, black lips pulling back from wet, white teeth.

Lieutenant Hubbard wrote his report with all the emotion of a popcorn fart.

Just like they taught him in the academy, just the facts:

> Training exercise for the day.
> Test firing of cannons.
> Drills proceeded without incident.
> Switched to live firing. All progressed as normal until rammer packed powder.
> Powder ignited. Reasons unknown.
> Cannon ruptured, killing all eight crew members and five additional soldiers.
> Review initiated.
> Findings forthcoming.
> Restate reasons unknown at this time.

*Distracted, bored. Nothing more to say. The report seemed thin. He
sat at his desk and fiddled with his pen. Drip go the minutes. He touched
the edges of the parchment in front of him, slid his fingers along the
creamy pages. He detachedly gave himself paper cuts on the ends of all
his fingers. Some bled. Some split callouses. Tick.*

Tock.

Drip.

*Lieutenant Hubbard pulled his coat closer around his shoulders. It
felt like cold lamp oil was seeping down his spine.*

Detail, halt!

*The men stopped and sighed. Breath blew from nostrils, horselike.
Plumes of foggy silver dissipated in the night's damp, and the troop
awaited further orders. Corporal Sprouse appeared confused; the men
watched his face closely. His eyes wandered to the tree line, then on up
the hillside where there'd been a lightning strike. Lonegan was none too
clear on where to begin the digging, and given the cedar and witch hazel
growing here, this ground he sent the men to scout was like to be far too
wet for proper burying.*

The corporal cut off a wad of tobacco and set to chewing.

*Lonegan knew what was coming, could sense this was going to be the
end for him and most of the men here tonight. Protocols. Rules. Death
has needs, too. The sergeant put down his pencil. Sealed up the letter.
Pulled two brass upholstery tacks from the old, wine-colored velvet chair
his last lieutenant gifted him, out of pity or respect he never could tell.
He held one of the tacks in his teeth while he rolled up his trouser leg
and then jammed the other long piece of shiny yellow metal through the
letter and deep into his right leg, the one made of wood, a gift from a
little trip to Mexico Lonegan took years ago, back when he had just
made sergeant for the second time. May the missus get hold of this when
they pull my body out of the shit pile, he thought. May the oldest boy
have sense enough to look after her. May the Creator make my journey*

easy, and may He take my hearing here shortly. He thumbed the other
tack, thinking. He knew he couldn't bear to watch so much death again.
What was one more glass eye on the off chance he didn't die, if Death
somehow spared him once again?

He ruffed the head of the nearest hound, the big red. It growled softly in
its throat, and smiled, just a little. He surveyed the camp at the bottom
of the hill. Lights dimmed in tents as his gaze swept from right to left
and back again. The hubbub of jokes and smokes and laughter and
cussing stopped abruptly. An inky silence enveloped the encampment.

Time to feed the dogs, he whispered.
   The screams began shortly thereafter and continued on through the
long, long night.

Jesusfuckinchrist, Teddy. What goes on inside that head of yours?
someone says.
   Someone else goes, What the fuck does Christ-All-Pee-Ickly
mean?
   Hahaha. I say it means like to turn something into gold.
   They say, Why the fuck do you know that? Why do you write shit
like that?
   One of us has got to, I say.
   Gooch laughs.
   I love your stories, he says.
   Fuck, man. Try having 'em in your head, I say.
   Better you than me, little brother, he says.

I clench, unclench.

THE LORDSPRAYER

MEMORY

for Gordon Henry

Truth in our stories
while maybe not "true," it is
what makes us ourselves

Truth, subjective sight
what we hear and say at night
salves rubbed on our souls

Truth, whispered aloud
stories told to sharp-eared friends
they know what we say

Truth, never quiet
asks for a voice, to be heard
persisting in us

In remain
    there's no main
unless we think
    of ourselves
        that way.

———

Our Father
who art
in the bar
came home one Sunday

I guess to watch the Cubs lose in the comfort of his own home. Maybe they were winning that year. It was '69 or '70—look it up.

He's home, and been drinking, so I want to go out and play.

If he's home, and it's day, and been drinking, I always want to go out and play.

Fake red and black Keds on—"base" and "ball"—one on each foot, shit in my pockets, check. Beer in one hand, Schlitz; smoke, Old Gold, in the other; something burning in the ashtray, check. Head down, cut through during commercial. "Nelson Brothers loves me, and they'll love you too."

Sizzzzzzzle. The newly focused stare drills into the back of my head.

Where ya goin'?

Outtoplay.

Really?

Guess so.

D'y'know the Lordsprayer?

What?

The Lordsprayer. Our Father who art in Heaven, hallowed-bethyname.

No. I guess not.

Well, when you do, you can go out and play.

Well. What the fuck is that? The Lordsprayer? I don't know what that is. And I say so.

The eyes focus. The Lordsprayer. Heathen. Little shit. It's the Lordsprayer. Your mother can teach you to read, but not the Lordsprayer? Jeeezus. It's in this book here, ever seen it?

This was a little black leatherine book I had never seen before. I thought I had seen all the books in the house. Boccaccio's *Decameron* on the bookshelf. Plato's *Republic* by the old man's chair. Plath's *Bell Jar* by Ma's stuff. But not this one. It was bendy and sweaty looking, as if it had only been perused in times of great stress, torn from a pocket and frantically searched for magic words.

Nope. I never seed that one before.

Well look right here. This is the Lordsprayer. You get that memorized, and you can go outside and play.

What?

That ain't a big fancy word for ya is it? *Memorized*. Yeah, *memorized*. When you get it *memorized*, you can go out and play. Tell me the whole thing, the Lordsprayer, get it right, and you can go out.

A photo from the '30s sits on my shelf at home, near to hand at my desk. It's my grandpa and his sister and their ma. Auntie looks like a big, wide, round-eyed Dorothy Dandridge, Grandpa looks a lot like a swanky Richard Gere as Dixie Dwyer in the *Cotton Club*, and Grandma Mary Josephine—well, she looks serene, but extra lively, and like she made both of them learn the Lordsprayer, with no small relish. This beautiful woman, white hair pulled back from her smooth and gorgeous face, sits between the two of them, dressed all in black, hands in her lap, gazing at unsuspecting viewers. Her own grandmother busted her ass to get her and her kids enrolled at Leech Lake, so you know she took zero shit, and it shows.

This amazing woman produced a son, who produced a son,

who was pissed when the Church made the switch from the Latinate mass; a Tridentine aficionado whose only visible use for a dead language in his life was to finish the crossword puzzle and win the occasional *Jeopardy!* round on the TV at the bar. But he was pissed. Remember when nuns were allowed to speak and the priests busted out the guitars and the kumbayas? Jeee-eee-eee-eeeee-zus Chrrrrrist.

I've never seen anyone so glad to get divorced and excommunicated in all my life.

So I know something about her, this Mary Josephine, *ina* and *unci. Omaamaa* and *nookomis.* Because I have her prayer book.

When Pop died, and they stole his eyes—and fuck you to my Christian-piece-of-shit uncle for letting them, I don't want to get things twisted in a Philbert Bono I-get-all-my-knowledge-from-*Gunsmoke* way, but fuck you Uncle if that evil anthropologist John Wayne was right in *The Searchers* when he shot out that poor old Noyeka's eyes and he had to wander forever between the winds, fuck you Uncle if my pop is out there wandering, but I don't think he is 'cuz when I dropped bundles for him and your dad and his grandpa and his grandma at the funeral I could see them all, all the relatives big and smiling in the sky at me from behind the headstones, I was the one who had to go to the old homestead and figure out what to do with his stuff, and that's right, by the way, fuck you too to the auntie for taking his dough out of the fridge and giving me a bucket of steel nickels with only one Indian Head that you missed, a bucket I still have and refuse to sell to good Ole Tom in East *or* West Hartford, ghouls all of you, you know his *wan-agi* walks around your house at night looking for a plate *and* his stuff you took.

His stuff. Man, there was a lot of stuff. He saved everything. He still had the fortune cookie slip that he filled out when he proposed to my stepma ("will you marry me? 2–14–81"). He had pictures he had drawn in school and a turtle he made when he was a little kid. Photos from when he went out west on a trip after high school to Arizona and New Mexico, and Old Mexico, places I think he wanted to move to but never did. His dad's wallet and passport. An article from the newspaper when a storm blew off the top of the house—they asked my grandma,

Didn't you wake up? The storm ripped the roof right off.

Mister, she says, I been sleepin' next to this man for forty years. I didn't hear nothin'.

Ho-lay!

There's a picture of him on his bike that sits in my house somewhere and that picture of his auntie and pa and grandma that I mentioned earlier. Beer coasters and drink mixers and pictures of us kids. I couldn't find the ever-dippin' googly bird and the red drink he eternally drank from—it was the only thing I ever bought off eBay—that I got for him one birthday, because Grandpa always had one there at the front entrance and the beak rotted away, so I replaced it.

Fuck you to whoever stole that.

See, when he passed, there was like a raid on the house. So disrespectful. But in there was the prayer book. That got missed, or left. Wrapped in an old plastic bread bag with much love by my Uncle Theo, who was my pop's uncle, and who he was named for. I'm a Theo Jr., so the name, like an itch, persists.

The prayer book has notes in it—and a four-leaf clover!—but the notes give an impression like she wasn't happy with the interpretations and devotions. This is a priest's book, but it's full of marginalia. Notes and dates with days when these things should be recited—very specific and structured. There's a feeling here that reminds me of Sister Leopolda in Louise Erdrich's *Tracks*, my favorite of hers, and that convert's struggle to outdo and outshame her betters and be a better Christian than those to the manor/

manner born, those who would never think to wear too-small shoes and burlap underwear to prove their love for God, or Jesus, or, even better, the Holy Ghost.

So I wanna go out. You wanna go out? Every little kid wants to go out. Especially if it's daytime and his Dad is drunk and the Cubs are losing again (I am a White Sox fan, by the way, just sayin') and it's too bright in the room and his eyes ain't focusing just quite right.

I take the sweaty little book.

Our Father, who art in heaven.

Our Father, who art in the tavern.

NO. That ain't it.

Our Father, who art in heaven,

some of you all are saying it. Well help out your neighbors there, and forgive them their trespasses, as we forgive those who trespass against us. You know the drill.

What seems like four hours later, but was probably more like forty minutes, sees me approach the old man.

I got it.

You sure?

OurFatherwhoartinheaven,

hallowedbethyname . . .

You know the drill.

I passed. My friggin' head was killin' me, but I did it. Little kid and all.

But something weird happened. The way I did it was to just look at it in my head and read it all over again. I didn't run the words together because I had crammed it all in there; I ran the words together because I was nervous.

So to show him I could do it, I did it twice.

And I told him the fucking page numbers, too.

18 and 19. I can *still* see them.

This lesson from my pop in memory, this exercise, a term I have heard again and again—"This prospectus is an exercise . . . These exams are an exercise"—is how I was able, at least as an undergrad in my late thirties when I still had that bear-trap ability, to tell my professor that Vizenor's quote

> Postindian autobiographies, the averments of tribal descent, and the assertions of crossblood identities, are simulations in literature; that names, nicknames, and the shadows of ances- tors are stories is an invitation to new theories of tribal inter- pretation . . .

appeared on page 1983 of the 2001 edition of *The Norton Anthology of Theory and Criticism*, whether I agreed with it or not, and was what made my eyes a little misty, when in my teens I first read a mention of our people, the Blackfoot Sioux, on page 423 of *Bury My Heart at Wounded Knee*, and how, just like in my grandpa's sto- ries he told me when I was eight, our people had to leave their chief because he no longer spoke for the people.

That memory of my old man and our time together is some- thing I never got to tell him about, or how I lost that memory because after I went to college I found out there were people called Native Americans, and I didn't realize I was one, or knew any, or would become one, and that he was one too, because where we came from, folks were just Indians back then. And we did what we did, and that was good enough.

Thanks, Pop.

GREAT AMERICA

L enny and Squiggy pull up.

They blurp the siren for a second. Maybe to startle me, but I already saw them coming. Maybe it's because their dads never loved them, never played baseball in the park with them. Or maybe it's because they're just dicks.

Whatcha readin' now, perfessor? Lenny says over the narc car mic.

I marched around with a stolen copy of *God is Red* stuffed in my pants most of that summer and part of the fall. It's my favorite Deloria. Sorry, Ravenswood Used Books. I owe you one.

I look at their greasy faces squinting over at me. They must've just come from lunch. Or they're sweaty from beating up JD or someone and they're hot because they never take off those cop leathers. Or they're teaching each other how to put on Chap Stick and they're not getting the hang of it quite yet.

The Bible, I say.

It shows me how to reach y'all's deepest fears.

Fuck you, you little shit, they say. Come over here.

Nah, I say. I'm kinda tired. Come visit. Set a spell. (I love the Beverly Hillbillies.)

They creak over my way. Gun holsters, big jackets, radios strapped to them. All that leather. Squeaking and snapping.

Whatcha readin' now, perfessor? Lenny says again, because it was so funny the first time, and makes like he's gonna punch me in the face.

Jackie Collins's *Hollywood Wives.*

I like the dialogue, I say.

How's yer ma? Squiggy says.

I just look at him. I breathe out through my nose.

I can't say nothin'. I chew the inside of my cheek with two of my dog teeth.

You know if we take you to jail right now and hold you until the end of our shift, she'll have to come pick you up for a curfew violation.

Fuck, man. Are you serious? It's like five in the afternoon, I say.

Yup. We're serious.

I pull a face like someone just crapped in the backseat. I make a sniff noise.

Problem? they say.

Something smell funny, asshole? says Squiggy.

I go, Desperation is an acquired taste, I suppose.

Lenny whacks me in the head.

Shit. They both liked her. Fuckin' weirdos. What am I supposed to do? I think.

Um, yeah. She's not around. She's on vacation with her boyfriend, I say.

Bullshit, says Lenny.

She ain't got no money for no vacation, he says.

Her boyfriend does, I say.

Lenny just looks at me for about a minute and then goes, Nah.

Ain't no money really in selling weed, says Squiggy.

He sells blue and clears, too, I say.

Tuinols.

Reds.

You lie, Squiggy says, grinning behind his aviators.

But we'll bust him later, they laugh.

Whatever. Fuck that guy, I say.

Oh, we will, they say.

And now you're going to jail.

Yeah. Give you a chance to memorize that dialogue you like so much.

Fuck, I say.

Fuck you, too, they say, and stick me in the back of the car.

We drive around for about an hour. They crack the window at least so I can smoke in the back. Don't burn nothin', dipshit, they say. It's a pain in the ass lighting matches and cigarettes and reading with the cuffs, and after I relentlessly bitch for about twenty minutes, regretting my recent read of *The Eighteenth Brumaire*, though still yelling about intraclass violence to these two and wanting my voice to drip with the disillusionment one would expect when encountering such disappointment, but just sounding wounded and sad at the fucking cops and their willful ignorance, they tell me shutthefuckup, they'll take 'em off in a little while. Shit. I hope so. I even pray a little.

Some call they actually pay attention to comes in over the radio. They huddle their heads together ("kiss! kiss! kiss!" I whisper/yell with just the right amount of sibilance to make it weird and unfunny) and then they grunt at each other for a minute or two. Lenny, he looks back at me with that look, and I'm like ahshitwhatnow? They pull the car over and throw it in park. Hop out of the doors and look in at me through the windows. Alright, I think. I'm getting out of here. Squiggy yanks open the door and pulls me out by the links between the cuffs. That shit hurts. And I drop my book. *Conan the Conqueror*. With the royal purple lettering and the Frazetta cover. You fucker.

Hold still, he says.

He takes the cuffs off.

Turn around, he says.

I turn around.

Snick, go the cuffs back on my wrist.

Goddamnit. Now what?

You're getting back in the car, Lenny says.

And we're going to pick up one of your buddies, Squiggy says.

Lenny goes, That fuckin' JD.

Yeah. He stole a gun.

We're going to get him, and you're coming with, they say.

Watch yer fuckin' head there, smiles Squiggy.

Shiiiiiiit, I say.

We peel out of the alley, gravel flying everywhere. Their total dickishness is on display as they laugh when the force from the acceleration throws me into the seat and tries to dislocate my behind-the-back handcuffed arms from my shoulders and I pull a face they can see in their mirrors, and I can see their faces back, those ones that watch everyday everything everywhere. I look from one side of the front seat to the other, consider my captors, contemplate the dickery they practice and impossibly attempt to enumerate its possible causes, 'cause these two are some grand assholes. Beat up in school when they were kids? No dates, no ladies? Some kind of repressed sexual weirdness? The violence that was always lurking, always present; that's what made me think this whole dyad we danced with the cops was just our gang versus their gang, and while they had some weapons and vehicular advantages, we had numbers and brains. And far fewer rules, if at least better morals.

It really did seem most of the time that it was just us against them, both sides steering clear of civilians, and us probably more than them always wondering where the other was. We were mostly good natured about our animosities and antagonisms; we thought it was pretty funny that time we threw a blonde-haired mannequin fifteen feet off the viaduct down onto its head in front of a squad car and had one of the peewees make the appropriate girl screams to accompany the jump, even if they didn't. Hahahaha. Holy shit— they were pissed. Jumped out of the squad car huffin' and puffin' like they were gonna kick the bucket on the spot. I thought, Shit, even I've seen folks die, and I'm like fourteen. What the fuck is wrong with these guys? And then they looked up and we were just laughing and laughing, crowded mouths all of us with sugar and Doritos and pop jammed in our teeth, hordes of decay waiting for us to pass out in the sun or the dark so they can get to work, strip away that one bit of whiteness we might still have, our only claims to royalty the crowns of enamel we're soon to lose. They tried to come get us, but they were too fat, and we tried to help by pointing out that fact:

Hahaha y'all fat motherfuckers. Come get us.

Look. They cain't get up the side of the tracks.

I think that one had a heart attack when the dummy hit the tar.

Shit. Looks like he dropped his donut.

Y'all ain't crying are ya?

Finally one of them figured out how to sideways crab that shit up the hill so we had to take off running. Fucking hilarious. I'm just glad he never squeezed off no shots, even if he sounded like he was about two minutes from it. I ain't never heard a cop cuss like that, well, maybe except for the one who crashed his car into the stanchion after we threw a mattress on him from up on the tracks. Now *that* shit was funny.

But *their* sense of humor? Nonexistent. I do think about some of the shit we did then, now, and well, yeah. I get it, I guess. There's a big difference between some kids skitching one-handed from the back of a CTA bus during a snowstorm, laughing at you and drinking from a gallon jug of vodka and giving you the finger while you're trying to maneuver your squad through black ice covered by piles of grey slush, versus dodging shots from an Uzi in the parking lot of a rib joint some sunny afternoon during a bogus dope deal and wondering what your kids will tell their friends at school the day after your funeral.

I think about that for a while. And I think about taking some notes on this exhausting day, like I should remember some of this shit. It's a good thing, too, because I do, and I find I need it later.

So, the English teacher says,

Today we'll have an in-class writing assignment.

Sort of a what-you-did-on-summer-vacation piece; a memoir, a reflection.

Be creative.

Be thoughtful.

Be handing me five hundred words by the time class is up.

Be handing me . . . I'm not gonna lie to you. She was a little bit crazy, but I think most high school English teachers should be, or will be. She always smelled perfumey. I never knew if it was incense or what, but I could see her hitting that weed and tryna cover it up for class. For sure. She had a crazy white lady fro and tons of big jewelry, probably a macrame owl in her kitchen too. Next to the harvest-gold fridge, right by the avocado stove. Above the pot plant in the windowsill. That she bought from some hippy at a festival in the park. Who she later had sex with. And was disappointed by.

So this is what I wrote. Five hundred words. Exactly. I was bored, so I went second person:

The rickety wooden rollercoaster makes you want to vom it. The sweat on your forehead doesn't even have time to dry, this thing is flying so fast. After the fucking bumper cars and the log ride, you're glad you drank whiskey instead of beer for breakfast. And at least you can smoke, if you sit in the last car.

Your ma and the rest of the class are tilt-a-whirling, or zippering, or skipping, or whatever the fuck you do at an amusement park. Playing hide-and-go-seek. You have your sights set on Alejandro, that fucking punk, that Corona. You can't believe your good luck that they decided on a field trip for all the classes, even for the gangbangers, Royals, sauly, Hooks, GDs. Normally you just glare at each other across the hall.

Awesome. Bugsfuckin Bunny. It looks like America exploded all over his face. This ridiculous outfit.

What's up, doc?

My foot in your ass, rabbit. Scram.

Awwww. Wittle wittle man has a big, bad attitude.

I mean it, jagballs. Keep it movin'.

A couple of the moms stare at you, but you head for the boat rides, give 'em the stinkeye and the hairflip. Light another smoke. It feels like you have bubble yum pulled over your face. Everything smells pink.

Halfway to the boat rides you stop by the food joints, hoping to raid a table or two. Grownups always leave their shit 'cause they never remember to get napkins. Or ketchup, for whatever the fuck those people eat. Sometimes there's a beer or two to be had. Just gotta be quick. Don't wanna have to turn on the waterworks unless you have to.

Well, well. It's Alejandro.

Hotdogs, cabrón? I knew you liked the weenie.

He doesn't see you yet.

Shit.

You can't let him see you.

You duck behind . . .

. . . this person. The aquanet/dippity-do/hairspray rolls off their head. You pull out your lighter, and . . .

Distraction.

*Pandefuckinmonium. The flames must be eight feet high. The initial
flash catches some greasy napkins and a bag of french fries. Fires start to
pop out everywhere, and polyester sizzles in the midday sun. That
fuckin' Tasmanian Devil spins by, fully engulfed. Hahahaha.*

Rawr.

(Please don't let the Big Red Monster catch me.)

*You snag an Old Style and kick back for a minute. This is better
than the Three Stooges.*

*Alejandro looks things over, grabs some lady's purse, and heads for
the edge of the park. It's either the Model Ts or the train. Fuck, you
think. I love trains. I hope it's the train.*

You light a smoke and lope along, never taking your eyes off him.

*Here's where it gets interesting for you. You could always do the shift
thing—there're enough fuzzy costumes here, and with the food court on
fire, you could do him and so easily slip back into your human skin.*

*But that would be too good for Alejandro. You decide on the knife,
because eighth grade, a lot like your teacher, is a real bitch.*

I got an A, and the weirdest looks you can imagine for the rest
of the school year.

Fuck, man. We've been driving around seems like forever. I'm getting the grand shithole tour of my own neighborhood. We're like
stopping to visit folks. Sure, I'm getting some great insights into
how very deeply sad Lenny and Squiggy's lives really are, but these
fucking cuffs are on way too tight. Goddamnit.

We pull over quick like on Clark Street near Chase. I can see
Claudia out of the corner of my eye, and apparently my captors can
too. Claudia is, of course, on the rag. I can see her paper bag from
here. Inside that paper bag is an old towel soaked in Toluene, and
she holds it to her sometimes-pretty face and inhales nice and
deep so she can get nice and high. And that is what they call being

on the rag around here. Not what you were thinking. And I think Claudia being on the rag is what actually keeps Lenny and Squiggy from buggin' *her* for blowjobs, because that Toluene'll make your eyes go all Barney Rubble, sure, but it'll also make you drool and lose control of your mouth and most of your face and all of your brain.

I guess we're just saying hi or something, because we pull right back into traffic.

We head north and then turn up Rogers Avenue.

Shit.

I know where we're going.

And they do too.

Squiggy yanks the wheel hard down Honore, and then we're headed the wrong way on a one-way street.

JD's house.

And you know he's there, too, the dipshit.

JD (run the J and the D together and say it "Jade") is the kind of burglar who stops every time and makes a fucking sandwich he's so predictable. And poor. Do you have any idea what it's like to be poor enough that you stop and eat something while you're doing a job?

Yup. Not only is JD home, he's sitting on his front stoop, smoking a cigarette and eating a sandwich.

For fuck's sake.

Get in the car, JD, they say over their car PA.

JD waves like oh yeah, and then

takes off running

behind his house

between his place and Rat's.

Lenny hops out of the car

(Whoa, I think, this must be serious)

and runs after JD.

Squiggy throws it in drive and lawn jobs the little strip of barely green grass between the sidewalk and the street and drives down the walkway after both of them.

Fuck, I think. This ain't gonna end well.

JD is running, eating his goddamn sandwich and taking drags off his cigarette.

He's almost to the alley and gone down the gangway when
I watch him slow
himself
imperceptibly
but just enough
to get caught.
He takes the last bite of his sandwich and prepares for Lenny,
who huffs and
puffs
and
punches JD dead in the stomach.
This huge cloud of smoke rolls out of him.
(Big man, Lenny, I think. We're gonna get you, fucker.)
JD goes down but doesn't drop his cigarette. I love this kid.
Lenny grabs him by the hair and shoves him toward us in the car.

Thought you were gonna get away, he says, thought you were gonna blahblahblah, he keeps going, blustering, running his mouth.

I tune him out. Big talk for a guy with a gun, a badge, and bad skin, I say to myself, but probably just a hair too loud.

What? Fuckin' punk, he says.

Nothin', I say.

Nice mustache, I say.

JD gets the cuffs, a punch in the face (*after* the cuffs, the big cowards), and then he's my seatmate. Lenny and Squiggy get whatever lame satisfaction they get out of this, plus JD's five bucks, Jimmy's mom's necklace, and Jimmy's dad's .357.

We take off driving around some more. Lenny and Squiggy congratulate each other for a while (and probs jerk each other off too, or would if we weren't stuffed in the back seat here) and kind of forget we're in the car. It's like being at home and they're our dads or something. We settle in and enjoy the day the best we can, chit-chat and whatnot.

Did you really steal Big Louie's gun, you dumbfuck? I say.

Shit, Teddy.

Well?

Yeah.

What the fuck is wrong with you, man? I say.

The violations are piling up on you, JD.

You're gonna take a hundred to the chest.

You're heart'll fuckin' stop, I say.

I'm sorry, man, JD says.

I forget his other nickname is Li'l Klepto, but that don't make it okay.

What the fuck, man.

They are gonna *beat* your ass, I say.

Shit, man, you still owe them fifty to the chest for that purse snatch the other day.

You're fucked, man.

I know, Teddy.

What am I gonna do, he says.

You're a crooked little fucker, that's for sure.

I don't know what you're gonna do. Shit. I don't know what you *can* do, I say.

I really fucked up, man, he says.

Did you at least shoot anyone? I say.

I did, Midget, he says.

Who? I say.

Alejandro, he says.

Fuck you, I say. Nay. You did not.

Ya, I did, init, he says.

No way, I say.

Where at?

In the back, he says.

Shut up, I say. No, *where* at, where did you see him?

That asshole was robbing T'n'T Liquors. I went in there to rob it, but that fucker was already doing it.

Hahaha, I laugh.

So what did you do? I say.

I let him finish, he says. And then I got the drop and robbed him.

I say, Nice. How did he get shot then?

After he gave me the money, I told him to leave the store.

Yeah?

And then when he was walking out I was like, well, I'll never get this chance again, so I shot him.

Is he dead?

He is now, he says.

What do you mean?

Well, after I shot him, I took off running, but the owner, that little Jamaican dude—

He's from Tobago, I say, T'n'T means—

Whatever, he says. The owner came out from behind the counter and blasted like five holes in him. If he ain't dead he'll wish he was.

Damn, I say. And then you just came over here and ate a sandwich?

Yeah, he says.

You're a cold-blooded motherfucker, I say. How much did you get?

Lenny and Squiggy perk up, look at us in their mirrors.

What are you two talking about? they say.

These fools can't understand our accents at all.

Nothing, I say, in theirs.

The price of tea in China, I say.

They pull over in an alley off Damen Avenue.

Probably talking about books, huh, perfessor? they say.

Yeah. That's it, I say.

What book now? they say.

Alvin Toffler's *Future Shock*. I like the premise.

Alvin what? they say.

Golding's *Lord of the Flies*.

I always look forward to the arc of the kid with the glasses, I say.

Pudgey! they say. We're going to get his fat ass, too. Take all three of you fuckers to jail. The first one of your moms who agrees to go out with us tonight—you get out of jail. You other fuckers can rot 'til morning.

Desssssssperation.

We'll be right back, they say, and get out of the car.

JD.

JD. Let's get the fuck out of here, I say.

Fuck you, Teddy. We're stuck, he says.

Whaddaya talking about, I say.

Do this, I say. Hop up off your ass and scootch your hands up under your legs.

Then you can bring your hands in front of you.

Not even, he says.

Watch, I say.

And I do it.

Hahaha, he laughs.

But yeah, dumbass, he says. We can't go nowhere no way.

Bullshit, I say. What do you mean?

The fuckin' doors are locked from the outside, Teddy.

You can't open the back doors in a cop car, he says.

I say, You're right, asshole. But this is a *narc* car.

It has regular doors.

See ya, I say, and open up my door and get out.

Holay. Wait for me, he says. JD does the hopscotch trick too, and then he's out in the alley standing next to me.

I reach in my pocket for my smokes and pull out my lighter.

Fuck, Teddy. Just hold on a minute. Let's get the fuck outta here first.

Fuck that, man, I say. Savor the moment, I say, getting my cigarette billboards all fucked up as I light a Kool. I say "savor," but I'm picturing the Newport one: "Es el sabor . . ."

Whatever, I say, to myself and JD both.

We take off down the alley, hustling a little but not running, because I refuse to be rushed.

Wait, JD says. How are we gonna get these cuffs off?

I ask him if he remembers *Cool Hand Luke* and the kid with the ax.

What, he says, his eyes all big and wide.

Nothin', I say, too tired from this day even to fuck with JD.

I say, Jimmy's got a key.

ON ICE

I remember when Clint killed this King on the Tracks. I say / we said "the Tracks," but that was really a name for this big section of the Chicago and Northwestern tracks from about Big Pit down to the stop at Lunt or so and meant all of this ground in between too. The Cinder Path, Pottawattomie Park, 3-D, all that, even the A&P's or the Aldi's or the National's or whatever it was called, the place where my brother, dusted out of his mind, took a sledgehammer to the cinderblock wall around midnight and finally broke in about four in the morning and got himself some goddamn beers. Which was better than the time he Batmanned through the skylight at the Community's or Zayre's or Ames or whatever because he wanted a bike and he got one and also the gumball machines that he had to throw off the roof four or eight times to get six bucks in nickels.

So yeah, this time that Clint shot this King in the head. I thought he shot him in the face the way the light was, but no, there was all this mess and this blood so for sure he shot him in the head and not the face. It was a quiet like night and we were just chillin', talkin' about things you know like what's up with your ma's new boyfriend I hate that motherfucker (ha! sorry) and he got weed though init and drinking beer not hurting nobody, not even mad that it was a little warm until it sat in the snow for a while. Just doing the talk. Of all the things. Green light to grey light to false dawn not-morning talking. We talked about a white kid we knew, this white kid adopted by a Native family, and you know we were just talking and that shit hardly ever happened, you know when you can talk to your friend and he don't make fun of you, you don't talk shit to him, ain't nobody judging, but you still have to be careful, you think, there's shit you won't say because just *maybe* that jagoff might use that shit on you later, but still, pretty cool. It's probably the only time you ever want to share secrets, and it's the one time in your life when you really can't. Maybe that's why it's so hard. Or maybe it's the dope. Anyway, it was just him and me talking and all cool like, you know, like when you're reading a book and it's just you and the writer, like that. There's always this secret between writers and readers and people never tell that secret either. They say oh yeah you should read that, it's cool, they never say and then he's talking about jerking off from the roof all over the city, not complainin' at all, or how the guy in the yellow coat rapes boys, or how you could turn yourself into a were-wolf if you really wanted or any of that shit. You all have got a secret now, you and the writer, and you cain't never tell nobody. Like that. That's the shit you wanted to have happen, the shit you wanted to talk about but never really could. You could get close. You could drink, and wanna open up, but usually you'd end up just punching the shit out of each other, 'cause that's how that shit works.

We're sitting there, talking, smoking 'ports, or maybe Kools, drinking these ever-colder Old Style tall boys, feeding this little fire between us, when I look up and see this dude coming across the ice. I say, Clinton, do you know this motherfucker? Nah, Teddy, he says, but he looks like a King to me. Huh, I say. Let him get closer. Fuck that—what the hell for? says Clint. He pulls out this chromed-up automatic with pearl grips. Holy shit.

We were just talking about Clint's ma's boyfriend. He laughed and said she calls him her fuckstick. I say, Who is he? He says, He's a fuckin' C$Note, some dude from like ChiWest or Taylor Street, he's an Italian motherfucker. He don't beat me up though, says Clint, and he's usually got dough in his passed-out pants pockets. Plus that weed, right, Teddy? I say, Huh. That's alright, I guess. I think about that word, fuckstick. Clint's momma's kinda big like, and I think that shit is nasty, can't imagine this Rico Suave jagoff goin' at his ma, but shit, someone got to pay the rent. And put gas in that '72 blue Newport Royal she hauls her ass around in. You know they moved in from somewhere else, 'cause they was the only fuckin' family in the neighborhood with a car. Also, Clint had this cool-ass shirt. It was just a white T-shirt but it had those short sleeves with extra material at the end that made the sleeves tight. I don't know why they did that, I think to make skinny guys feel like they had muscles, but it said playboy playboy playboy playboy all over in this turquoise color, and after each playboy playboy playboy playboy it had a 🐰 🐰 🐰 🐰 in turquoise too. I thought, man, that shirt is the coolest, even if he wore it every day. All that playboy. All those bunny heads. Those bunny heads made you think about how every magazine cover had a hidden bunny head. And those covers, well they made you think about what was inside. And all of that made me think of the last time I went to class. That was a while ago, but when I was there, I couldn't pay attention to my work 'cause of my lab partner, or maybe the weed. Nah. It was Lenore. Dang . . .

Lenore. That one day I was looking at you in Miss P's horticulture class, and I was like damn you are so beautiful, lookin' like I don't even know who but even better and you got it goin' on and that body and all, but Lenore, 1955 called and said whoa what's up with that hairdo? Right this way, young lady, we're going to need you to be our grandmamom, 'cause that is the oldest old lady fade we have ever, ever seen. And that's the problem with gettin' high at school, shit, that's the problem with gettin' high period, at least for me, see? You ain't never serious. Cain't work, cain't spell, and cain't mack on the girls at school. Got no game. Just talk shit and crack jokes that prolly ain't even funny. Man. Sleeping on the opposition will get you killt anyway. Or at least shot up. No room for the weed in my life.

And that's the story I wanted to tell Clint, but I didn't. And I didn't tell him what it felt like the other day when I stole this bike and raced that shit down Clark Street, and I went to the comic book store 'cause I had a little money, and I bought the new Hulk and stole the new X-Men and a Thor and would've gotten the new Conan except I couldn't find it, and then I hopped back on that bike and it was warm and this long-ass hair I got was all streaming out behind me as I stood up on the pedals and the opening chords to Barracuda blasted out of this one storefront and I was never, ever, ever gonna die. But because this boy's life is what it is, I just said some stupid shit like, Yeah, if that bitch ever gets out of hand or treats your ma bad we will fuck. him. up. and Clint laughed and said, Fuck, Teddy, that motherfucker would just as soon shoot you as give you the time of day so I wouldn't worry about it if I was you, Midget, and then he looked down the sight on that automatic and squeezed off two shots, quick like, while he said plow-plow out loud, and they panged off the ice and that King looked up and he started running.

Clint sets down his beer and takes aim with both hands.

Shit, man. Twenty minutes ago Clint came back from grabbing up some chunks of wood and bark and shit from a clump of birches on the side of the tracks about thirty feet away, down and up from the first-base line of diamond two at Pottawattomie. We had just come back with our stuff from doing a cart at the National's (I don't know why this is, but in Chicago the grocery stores all end in a possessive "s," as in "go get some fuckin' milk from the Jewel's or the

Dominick's or the IGA's or the Hi Neighbor's). We used to do this pretty regularly at the National's. We would put a bunch of beer in the bottom of a shopping cart, then load it up with shit that we wanted, like lunch meat or hot dogs and bread and tortillas and mustard and whatever, then a couple of us would wait outside while a couple of us just shoved that motherfucker under the bar and turnstile thing by the front doors. The cart would trip the automatic doors and keep rolling on through out to whoever was waiting for it. They would grab all the shit out of the cart and then run through the parking lot to where we had cut a hole in the chain link fence by the steepest part of the hill heading up to the tracks at the top, and then they'd haul ass down the tracks with the beer and whatever else they could carry out of the cart. Then we'd all meet up, usually behind the Jackass leather place, and get to grubbing and drinking. Sometimes, in the summer, if we had Brain with us, we could talk him into going back inside and using his food stamps to buy ice for the beer, which was always warm.

So, a little bit about Brain. This dude was this massive, hulking, Howard Street Lord, who, for some reason, didn't get along with his set anymore. I remember humbugging with the Lords, and that motherfucker would be there, and I was always like, man, I need to put space between me and that fucking guy; he looks like on that one Bugs Bunny where Bugs takes the nasty Dr. Jekyll formula and transforms into a giant rabbity Mr. Hyde. Yeah. That's exactly what this dude looked like. And, bonus, he was obviously mentally unbalanced, and I ain't saying that just because he was like nineteen and gettin' food stamps. I'm saying it because one day we were sitting around drinking after Brain had come back with some ice (Brain! I'm the Brain! I get the ice! he would say) and he goes, Yeah, winter is coming. I like that. Why, Brain? we say. That motherfucker goes, Well, because it gets darker earlier. And I got more time to rob people when they get off the El.

Jeezuschrist.

So yeah, Clint and I had just done a scaled-down version of the cart roll, just beer though, not even stuff for sandwiches and whatnot, and we're chilling the beers in the little snow piles that are left on the side of the tracks in late March and getting a little fire going in a pit we've dug. It's a pretty warm night, but the wind is picking up a little and it's gonna get cold, but for now we can see the water running on top of the ice in the field under what was left of the high arc lights we were always busting out. Pottawattomie is a big park with three baseball diamonds and a huge football field, and the white guys who ran it were always trying to get us to do stuff, like wrestling, or tumbling, or *something*. They thought maybe we should be like them, and like hockey, so they iced down a big section of the field. We liked hockey okay, I guess, but we liked the sticks best of all, so those just kind of disappeared, and then no more hockey, but we still had all the cuts and bruises we would've gotten if we would've played instead of just beaten the shit out of each other, and maybe even learned something. But no.

Clint pops off a shot. It hits the guy in the foot. I see him jump and try to grab at it to look, but he just keeps running. I'm like, Hmmm, that's not bad, Clint will just let him go. It can't be too bad anyway. Well, at least it's not like in the movies where *plow!* someone gets shot and *bam!* down they go, another body in the alley. It makes me think of this time years later when I was bullshitting with these two buddies of mine that worked the door at this punk rock bar on Milwaukee Avenue we all worked at (I was a bartender), standing around out front before the rush, having a smoke, taking a break, and this stupid yuppie/jock/fratboy comes up and starts telling us how he's been shot—I've been shot!—and we're like, Yeah, whatever. No, for real! he keeps saying, so I'm like, Okay, where? and he goes, Here in my leg. I look at the front of his leg next to the shin about two inches below the knee in his fat, fat calf and I see all this blood soaked into his pant leg and I think, Yup, he's probably been shot, that's a lot of blood, and I look on the other side of his leg and, cool, yup, same thing, tons of blood, so I say, Let me see, and he goes, See, right there! and I say, Mmmhmm, and I stick my pinkies in the holes in his leg under the pants and he goes, OWWHATTHEFUCKAREYOUDOING, and I say, Man, it's a through and through, you'll be fine, don't go to the hospital though unless you want to tell the cops how and why you got shot, and, oh, by the way, how did you get shot? I need some water, man, he says, and I say, What were you doing that you got shot? and I give the head nod on the water to the fellas, and he says, Well, I was trying to buy some weed. Mmmmhmmm, I say. Where at? Over in Wicker Park, he goes. That's the actual park a block over from where we're chitchatting that he's referring to, not the now-gentrified neighborhood of the same name where said park is located. I say, Did you actually pay for it, or did you try to beat them out of paying? He says, Well, I shorted them a little. How much? I say. 'Bout half, he goes. I say, Well, then you deserved to get shot. Here's your water ya dumb motherfucker, Sleazy says. Spanky goes, Now get the fuck out of here, dipshit. I say, Later, dumbass, and, Direct pressure is your best friend. We go back to telling jokes and making fun of Bob for a while and then I have to get back inside and wait on the fucking yuppie tourists.

Me and Clint wrap it up, I guess. We gotta run down this corona and finish the job. Fuck. I do *not* want to walk away from all this beer. I cover it up as best as I can using a bunch of leaves and snow and shit, but I still worry someone'll creep up and find our stash. I know it happens, and I'm a little skittish anyway. Man, there was this one time I had stashed a half bottle of crème de menthe on the tracks. It was like eight in the morning, and it was bright, and already really hot and humid, and I just couldn't drink anymore. I needed to crash for a minute, so I was like fuck it. I'll just hide this shit behind Sergio's. By this time the Jackass leather place had gotten bought up by Sergio and turned into a gym, but we still called it Jackass, but not because of Sergio. Sergio was *that* Sergio. "The Myth." Mr. Olympia. The only guy to beat Schwarzenegger in a Mr. Olympia contest, and the only cop I could stand. He was a good guy. I always thought he was particularly good to us longhairs, and now that I think about it, maybe that's because the village in Cuba he was originally from had a long history with Indians. And the Jackass leather company? Fuck those guys. They made holsters out of *horse*hide for the CPD and those other assholes on *Miami Vice.* And they threw out all their fuckups and trash on the tracks behind their stinky factory and then moved to Phoenix or something. Suck it. I wrapped the bottle up in this big old brown paper bag and stuck it in this little ditch in the side of the hill behind Jackass.

I came back later in that late afternoon / early evening / magic light time of day with my brother (no dust or burglaries *that* day, at least not yet) and one of his friends and one or two of the Jimmys. Cool. I was like, It should be right over here. They gave me the yeah right looks but followed along anyway. I said, There's at least half a bottle. We can get buzzed and go do a cart or something. Or head down to Farwell and see what's up. Hold on. Here it is.

Sure enough, I found the paper bag. I reached down and picked it up. It was super wrinkly and felt kinda damp, but whatever. Like I said, it had been hot and humid all day, so . . . yeah. But then I noticed it felt light. Shit. I went to open the bag and what? Dang it smelled funny. Huh. Shit. Okay, I thought. Let's see. Hahaha. I opened it up and the bottle wasn't in there. Whatthefuckisthis? Instead, I'm looking at a lump of black fabric. I pulled that shit outta there and goddamn. It was a fucking Batman suit. Holy shit. I threw it out on the ground and, yup, a mask fell out with it. We all looked at each other like whu . . . I could feel though that there was something still in the bag. I eeped my face over the top, eyes slowly rolling down, and . . . what? There was a big, used dildo in the bottom of the bag. I laughed and flung it at my brother's buddy. It hit him in the face with a *thwap* sound and then we were all laughing. Shiiiiit. His face turned red, even redder than where I hit him in the face with the dildo, and we were just dying and shit. Fuck you! he yelled, and we're all just, yeah, we can't even talk. I imagined this Batman prick, drunk on crème de menthe, chasing people down the alley next to the tracks, slinging his dildo around, yelling, Holy Strap Ons! and doing lord knows what to the people he caught.

So yeah, I'm careful and nervous about hiding stuff on the tracks, but I got no choice and no time because Clint's on the move, hustling down the side of the tracks to go get this hijo de puta. Who the hell is that, man? I ask him. I don't fucking know, Teddy, he says. Let's just get him. Shit. He's moving again. Goddamnit, Clint says. He pops off another shot, and I see the guy go down like he's dead. Feet fly out from under him and he falls straight back. I can hear this loud *thunk* sound when his head hits the ice. Me and Clint move a little slower. We look around, but the whole park is deserted. One or two cars way far away in the parking lot that have been there I think since they built the place. A bus, one of those new double ones, goes by on Rogers Avenue just past the lot. But no cars. No people. Nothing. We roll up slow and cautious. Dude is not moving. At all. Laid the fuck out. Hands flung straight from his sides, feet angled almost heel to heel, showing black Converse hi-tops with gold laces. Clint sees them too and spits on the guy. We look around one more time, and then down at this King, this pinche puto lying in a dark, dark puddle.

But all that blood and whatnot? Man, we can see this asshole had just slipped and cracked his head open. We could hear him breathing, for Chrissake. Clint couldn't shoot for shit. I don't think he even hit the dude's foot. Nope. Nothing there at all. Dude must have been hopping along to check it like he couldn't believe he missed either. We sweated walking up to this corona laid out on the ice, big puddle of blood all blooming around his head. We even habla ingles puto?'d and all that shit, but dude was just passed the fuck out. Clint was gonna kick in his ribs or piss on him or something, but I was like, Nah. Just leave him there. Think about what it'll be like when he wakes up and the back of his head is frozen to the ice.

You're a cold motherfucker, Teddy, he says.

And we slip and slide back to our spot on the tracks.

BUMBLEBEE AND THE CHEROKEE HARELIP

want to start this out in a particular way, and I have a note to help me; it reads, "Maybe she didn't love me so much, but she loved my dad." How do I know she loved my dad, other than the fact that she talked about him for longer than she was married to him? Let's ask *The Cherokee Harelip*. Period. Don't forget the period. And yeah, it's in bold in the notes.

Ha.

It's supposed to be about, or start out about, a time in Michigan, which for me if I'm just little means it's summer. Ever been to Michigan in the summer? Central Michigan, in the crotch of the thumb—the place you lick salt from when you're drinking tequila the fancy way, or where you sniff coke from in the bathroom of the bar in between those rounds of drinking tequila, if you're so inclined, or have the dough, or the connect—yeah, that part of Michigan? One of my uncles told me once when I was about fifteen how hot it was. And you all know the line and are saying to yourselves, How hot was it? He allowed it was hotter than a dead raccoon's cunt. Sound hot? Yeah. And it's humid, too.

The thing about this story is, I was actually too young to

remember it, and so I only know this story like my ma told it to me. It's hard to get stories out of her. Not because she doesn't like to tell them, or because I don't talk to her no more, but because she can't tell stories without laughing. Now I'm not saying she wasn't funny sometimes, well, okay, lots of times, but seriously, she would laugh and laugh and snort—ha, she'll be pissed if she ever reads that—and smoke and tell these stories.

Central Michigan means Bay City, Essexville, the Quanicassee, Munger, Saginaw, Midland, Fairfield, Hampton Township, and Frankenmuth. Not because Frankenmuth is handy, but because I always remember one of my great-uncles had an icebox full of Black Label, and they make it in Frankenmuth. And because one time one of my other uncles came and picked us up and we drove in the middle of the night and he was like, Hey, let's stop in Frankenmuth, I know this shortcut, but we all had been drinking a lot and so we only saw some deer and our breath hanging over a fallow cornfield as we pissed in the night on the side of the road and wondered how we ever got so lost.

I'd like to talk about how one day we were driving with one of my other uncles, the weatherman there from earlier, down the Quanicassee, when he slams on the fuckin' brakes and tells me, Quick! get out of the pickup and help him with this fuckin' thing, and he takes a baseball bat and him and my cousin lower it down and *clamp!* they pull up the biggest snapping turtle this city boy's ever seen and they throw him in the back and we drive to this other guy's house and he hits him with the bat and then he rips off the shell and says, Did you know there's seven kinds of meat on a turtle and we're gonna eat good. But I won't, 'cause we've got some other shit to talk about.

What were we talking about? Oh yeah. Bumblebees. And Cherokee harelips.

Can we talk about one without the other? I don't think so. Not now, at least. Both have roots in Michigan, Central Michigan that is, a place I think that is or should be separate from the rest of the state. We have to talk about Cherokee harelips so we can talk about my ma. She's Cherokee, but she's not a harelip. And she's not from Michigan, Central or otherwise. She's one of those Cherokee-hillbillys from East Tennessee—Blount County. She told me one time that she went back to see the old places. And she told me the saddest story about how the houses are gone, along with our genealogy, which got stole by some Yankee fuck tourist out of one of the houses that the Feds turned into some kind of living museum or human zoo exhibit in the national park that sits where our land used to be, but the flowers remain, rectangular plots of flowers that still grow around the perimeters of long-ago houses that have burned into ashy pages of lost history. But she didn't laugh during that one.

Remind me to talk about the picture of my ma's grandma—she looked like Esther Rolle—and how my ma put that picture away, for reasons we'll discuss later.

I have to talk about cousins for a second. Talktalktalk, I know. We have a pile of cousins up there. I have like twenty-seven first cousins of my own on that side of the family. We also have some Sag Chips, redheads, and Mexicans. And some Van S(Z)oomerings, and dude don't you know, we're driving around in this maroon, well okay NDN Red (question—do they make that color in the Crayola box anymore, maybe in Europe? 'Cause one day in an undergrad Native lit class I took I was like, Hey, everybody—hold up them books. What color are all the covers? And they were like, Uh, maroon, and I said, No. They're Indian Red. Do they even make that color in the Crayola box anymore? Hahaha. That's some OldManNDN talk right there, son) 1968 Chrysler Newport drinking out of pint bottles with my dad's cousin Ronnie Van S(Z)oomering and on the radio is the Zombies' "Time of the Season" and that smelly drunk cousin of ours with adult cradle crap in his hair and the weird smell and the shy eyes behind the birth-control specs and the funny laugh pops in my head whenever I hear that song and I always think of him as Ronnie Van Zombie, even when I heard a cover of the tune by a hair metal band at the Whiskey when I lived in LA—whoa that was fucked up. It works out, because like us, half of the cousins are Indians and the other half ain't. Or something.

So now you're going what the fuck and you're like that French trapper from the 1600s who wrote back to that europissoir known as Paris in his journal something along the lines of, "These people (yeah, even back then, "these people") are the most circumlocutory individuals one would ever want to meet. I find myself again and again, as we discuss first the state of my family, and then the varying states of their families and relations, wondering if we will ever get down to business, and usually after the space of three or four days, we do," or some such thing. Well *plus ça change* people. We're gettin' there. Besides, I write fast, don't I?

So my ma, who would dress me and my brother in the latest little-kid-hippie-dork fashions, much to the horror and dismay of my grandma, and the grating, sighing, and studied indifference of my dad, who could find any number of reasons to begin drinking after lunch and didn't need the indignity of his oddly dressed sons to provoke a pre-twilight bender, would sit at the table and beat barbs and brows with Grandma, each blowing smoke in the other's face, Lucky Strike versus Old Gold in a titanic death dance, matching cup for cup of coffee chugged from melamine cups in turquoise and pumpkin, oleo tubs of lunches—whoops, "dinners," we're in Michigan, not Chicago—of leftover potatoes and pot roast crusting over under the searing weight of their combined contempt for one another.

Dad and Grandpa, taking their cues and their keys, head out to

Phil's, small-town precursor to Cheers, where everybody knew everybody's name and business and thanked God or whoever they chose to thank that Grandpa's son is the county sheriff and that he can pull him out of the ditch later on when they've all gone home, beneficiaries of those two legendary barmen's largesse and good-will, qualities they always chose to spend on their fellow patrons rather than their fellow family members.

But dude—don't think the bar thing is completely a bad thing—Grandma used it to pay for Christmas. Hey, Grandma. Is that Maxwell House can really full of money? Oh ho, she'd say, it is. Where'd ya get all that money, Grandma? From Grandpa's pockets. I do the wash. And Grandpa thinks he has a good time every night. At least that's what his empty pockets tell him. Jesus Christ I miss my grandma.

Are you doing this thing now, where you're going, "Hey, is Phil's the place where we learn more about the harelip?" or, "I wonder if his grandma is going to tell him to stay away from harelips, and that's where it's going to come in," or, "I bet you he tells us some other shit, like how he's singing along with Ibrahim Ferrer on 'Todavía Me Queda Voz' while he's writing this, instead of what we want to hear, which is about the harelip."

Dick.

It's not going to come from my grandma, because she didn't know about the girl harelip, though she knew about the boy harelip, but he comes in later, and none of her kids were harelips. Grandma had eight kids, and it was like a genetics class. She had two dark ones with black hair and black eyes, two dark ones with black hair and blue eyes, two light ones with dark hair and blue eyes, and two lighter ones with dark hair and dark eyes. When my daughter was born after my grandma had passed my aunties did the variation of what I heard our Spanish neighbors do when a light-skinned baby was born, except our family would say, "Oh, she would have loved your daughter. She always liked the light ones with the dark hair and blue eyes."

You have to understand that this was something of no small import for them. I remember once my ma telling me this story about my Aunt Jessie. She was out working on her tan—ha! She was dark like a walnut!—at the edge of one of the fields that her husband's family owned. Kicked back, relaxing, with maybe a radio (but probably not originally sinning with INXS, probably more like hearing from Ronnie Milsap about how we ain't gettin' over him) and some lemonade, when this white foreman runs over hollerin' and swearin', something like, Hay tambien muchas mas ojas, hija de puta, get to work, ondele, trabajar bitch, etc. And she's like, What the fuck is this cracker talking about, except she said, Hey—my husband's family owns this property, mister, and so he had to quick like turn around and try not to swallow his Skoal on the spot and instead goob it up in the field there. So, yeah. It was important.

And though there were a lot of us kids, I like to think that we were important. And of course we all like to think we are important, especially in the eyes of our family.

A couple of years ago, I gave a presentation on Sherman Alexie's film *The Business of Fancydancing*. It was at the Saginaw Chippewa's Soaring Eagle Casino. Wait. Shit. I hate when this happens.

I was talking to some colleagues the other day. We were talking about . . . you know, honestly I don't remember what the lead up was, but somehow it was related to counterfeiting. And I was like, Hey, I remember . . .

Well what I remembered was this.

I told them about this roommate of mine I had a long time ago. We shared an apartment up on the North Side of Chicago, all the way up in Rogers Park. It was off of Devon Avenue. A decent area, I guess. One of those buildings that when I was a kid I used to hit the laundry machines in the basement with a crowbar and clean out all the quarters. And steal the pop bottles off the back porches so I could go to the movies with my friends on Friday. But I didn't tell them that. Or about how the main dude, who was taking correspondence courses to become a private dick, hocked my Gibson EG to pay the rent one day.

Anyway, I lived in this apartment with a couple of other guys, Nubby and Foos. Nubby was the pawn shop aficionado and Foos was . . . something else. An electrician, dealer, and counterfeiter.

One day there was a knock on the door.

Who is it?

US Secret Service.

Hilarious. Who is it?

Secret Service.

Ha. Like James West and Artemis Gordon?

You're hilarious. Open the fucking door.

Dude. Seriously. It was the Secret Service.

And I know you're thinking, What about a warrant? Warrant? This is fucking Chicago we're talking about. Warrants. This is the place where one day I was running down the alley from the cops and this GI (Gang Intelligence) pops out of the side of a building and says, C'mere, Injun; grabs me by the hair and throws me over the hood of a car. And then . . . Never mind. We've already got enough threads to hang on to right now.

Do you know where Foos is?

I just live here, man. And mostly only in the back, anyways. See that pile of laundry with the sheet on top? That's my bed. I never see him.

What do you got going on in here? They peek around the corner.

Nothing. Seriously. It's dull. We don't even have a TV.

Where do you think he is?

Fannie May?

The mortgage office?

I don't know.

You're funny. You got any money, any C-notes on you?

No, I thought. I only deal in twenties and fifties.

Nope.

Do you know where this big fat fuck Bill is at?

Dude. I don't really like fat people.

Go back to bed. If Foos shows up, tell him to call us.

Uh, yeah. I'll get right on it. 1-800-WildWildWest, right?

Hilarious.

Holy shit. Thumpthumpthump. Our apartment was full of shit. Everywhere. There were enough crumbs of shit on the floor to start a full-scale Columbian riot. Long story, and not one for here, but, yeah. If those guys wanted to be dicks and call the narcs, well, shit.

So I had this talk with Foos. Turns out it's hard to pass hundred dollar bills. But one of the best places to do it is at candy stores. You know, the high-end ones. And that's what they were doing.

Man, I was pissed. Not that they were counterfeiting and shit. Who gives a fuck about that, right? No. The Secret Service showing up at the door is not cool. How to express my displeasure?

Remember, Foos is a dealer. And it's the '80s. Dude, I used to page him three or four times a day. I'd leave numbers to the Chicago field office of the FBI. Regional DEA. CPD Gang Intel. We'd run into each other in the kitchen. Two eggs and six ketchup packets in the fridge. Suppertime.

You think that's fuckin' funny, asshole?

What?

The pages to the man.

I couldn't help myself.

How fuckin' stupid are you? Ain't you got no retention, man?

You can't recognize a number after calling it three times, your ass deserves to get locked up.

Wanna get high?

Yeah. Whatever.

So yeah. The conference. I gave a paper on Alexie's film *The Business of Fancydancing*. My aunties show up, and . . .

I'd like to talk about these things, but I can't. So I'll write 'em.

So the aunties come to the conference.

Will they let us in?

Do ya think it'll be okay?

You should ask them . . .

Thanks, Gwen. Two aunties and a cousin come over to the casino. And we're listening to one of my co-presenters . . .

Zzzzzzzzzzzzzzzzzzzzzzzzzzzzzzzzzzzzzzz.

Aunt Janey, out like a dog in a patch of sun.

I can't wake her up, right? But she keeps goin', ya know? So I give her the nudge.

Mmmmmm hmmmmmmm.

God almighty, she sounds just like Grandma.

We get through that presentation, and I'm up.

I'm going to read:

"Talking Circle": Speaking With and Without Reservation(s) in *The Business of Fancydancing*.

I say, I'd like to briefly let you know that there's some salty language in this paper and the clip from the film. And since I have some aunties in the audience—. . . , . . . , . . . Aunt Janey, all the swear words are Sherman Alexie's and not mine . . .

Afterward, they laugh and say, Holy crap. All that talking you did when you were a kid . . . and now you get paid to run your mouth. And they look at me in my sport coat with my name tag and they say, Geez. We're proud of you.

I wanna friggin' melt.

Then Aunt Janey says, I'm taking you to lunch. When she says anything, you don't mess. She actually got my son to finish his supper one time. And for a couple of *years* all I had to do was mention her name and that plate would be clean. So off we go to lunch.

I think I've got a discount ticket or something here, she says.

We get to the buffet and she daintily takes out this black card and hands it to the dude.

He says, Right this way, Mrs. Howard.

Come here often, Aunt Janey?

Mmmmmm hmmmmmmmm.

. . .

Shiiiiiiiiiiiiiit. We paid off two cars outta this place. Monthly payments. They've been trying to get their money back ever since.

. . .

Mmmmmm hmmmmmmmm.

Jesus. The harelip already.

Fine.

My dad told me that his best friend growing up was this dude with a harelip. They went everywhere together, did all kinds of shit and generally got in trouble together. Best buddies and all that. My dad also told me about his first girlfriend down in the city, back home now.

Jesus, Speedy. She was beautiful. But nobody would ever hit on her because they couldn't understand her. I took one look at her and I was like, Wow. So I talked to her. Mnhay. Mnhow nya ndoin? 'Cause that was Pop. And that's how he told me the story. He told me other stuff she said, and he said, but like "Hey baby" stuff, and I don't want to talk about that here.

Anyway, they move in together, right away. He allowed things were great. He says, She could've been your mother. Shiiiiiiiiiiit.

And then he met *my* mother.

There used to be a diner on the corner of Montrose, Sheridan, and Broadway in the little triangle there. My ma was a waitress there. My dad used to bartend down the street. I know how the bartending thing works in Chicago; you're not supposed to drink while you're on duty, but you basically are getting paid to host a party. And you drink. And my dad would drink at a kid's birthday party, or a funeral, or at breakfast. So, whatever. He was drinking.

One night he goes into the diner, shit-faced. And he passes out. In a bowl of chili. Face down, he starts to drown. Remember that story about on the rez, guy dies in a two-inch puddle of water? Well you can do the same thing in four fingers of chili in the middle of the city.

My mom grabs him by that luscious black hair that he used to wear an onion bag on like some freaky Indian do-rag and saves his ass from drowning. It was love, or a semblance thereof, at first blurry sight.

They hit it off great, I guess. Or at least my ma thinks they do, 'cause at the time she's living in the Horseshoe Projects, the Lathrope Homes at Diversey and Damen. And guess what? Yeah. She wants to get the fuck out of there.

There's only one problem. She can't move in with Ted Sr. 'cause there's already someone living there. So Eastern versus Western, my ma goes to my dad's house and whirlwinds old girl's shit out the window, down the stairs, and into the street. My dad would laugh like he was getting paid to do it every time he told me the story.

Speedy, he says, she walked into my apartment and was like, Bitch, you won't need this shit no more, and just started wingin' her stuff out the windows and into the hallway. Shiiiiiit. She was in love.

And she was, too, bwai. Like I said, she talked about him twenty years after they split up like they still lived together. Crazy.

Alright. So that's the harelip story. But where's the bumblebee?

Ahh, yes. My fierce mother.

So one day she's pushing me in the stroller. On the grass, in the front of Grandma and Grandpa's house. I know. A stroller. On the grass. Hey, we're from the city. Whadda ya want?

She's walking along, hippy clothes, black beehivey do, and I'm sure Grandma's glaring out the window somewhere inside the house. My ma says to me, This big fucking bumblebee, like the size of a tennis ball (and of course I always thought that's how big they were—to this day when I hear the word "bumblebee" I think of a big yellow-and-black-striped ball with a little head on top) comes out of nowhere. And . . . what could I do? I sort of pushed you by this tree and I took off running.

Imagine my mother, twenty years old, freaky striped pants, cat's-eye glasses, and crazy-ass jet-black beehive hairdo, abandoning her baby and running, running through the grass, going God knows where. Just running.

Shiiiiiiiiiiiiiiiiiiiiiiiit.

JUST MARQUEE

Choochie says, C'mon, Teddy. Let's get these fuckers.

We head down Clark Street, *our* street, Farwell and Clark Street, F/C, site of lots of young gangbanger triumphs (and whoa, wait, we should clear that up pretty quick like—"gangbanger" here just means "gang member," containing zero hints of any more nefarious connotations implied by that rhymey and angular term that can mean so much sexually and violently and so little socially all at once) and also a library. A Chicago Public Library. Site of much theft and pillaging, much pilfering, of knowledge, of words, and of Conan books. Definitely those. Oh. And a *Beowulf*. That's right. 'Cause fuck those Geats.

Anyway, it gets funky because now only one block down and two blocks over it's C/A, Columbia and Ashland, with a new branch of sᵻuⱤ (ʞk). What the fuck. And yeah. Fuck those sᵻuⱤ. Hector and them, yeah, but shit. These other fuckers. Not even Montrose and Hazel. We don't know who these guys are. Choochie says we should take some of them out. He ain't kidding. Choochie has given zero fucks since eighth grade, which is when he dropped out of school. It's on. Son of a bitch.

We wait 'til it's like a Thursday night or something. I think Thursday, because it felt like a Thursday night in the way that Thursday night is really just Friday eve and kind of stays that way, at least until you're old, like in your forties or whatever, whenever your future old lady can make you stop going to the bar.

It's Thursday eve. We meet up by Choochie and Julius's house, down on Farwell. We get blowed as fuck; Choochie has dumdum sticks he got from Jimmy. Holy crap. We have a dude in the neighborhood who works at an undertaker's, one of those ones like on Southport or Ashland or something, in the cool old buildings that look like museums but aren't museums, but now that I think about it, kind of are museums, but with premature mummies instead of the crusty old wrap jobs like at the Oriental Institute, where we would have to go on field trips sometimes, and he can get us the formaldehyde. You dip joints in it and smoke them after it dries. Yeah. High as fuck.

We sit around for a while and talk shit. But really high shit, so I don't remember too much of it. I remember making fun of Muck (well not really, but you know I could just say that anyway, and it would be true about 99 percent of the time), and then talking about who was in jail (mostly Howard Street Greasers), who was out (Goof, who had a new tattoo of a .45 on his arm and some pants he liked), who was probably gonna end up going in (Frankie. Definitely Frankie), and who was due to get out (not many folks, and definitely none of the Grease, 'cause those guys were all like thirty to life). That seems to be about all the shit you talk about then, because that's all you really can talk about. The how does that make you feel, and what do you think when your friend goes to jail, all that talk is for social workers and the guys who run the field house for the park district and who try to get you all to wrestle or do tumbling and shit. We don't talk about that stuff.

I'm over at the payphone by the library. Muck, Julius. A couple of the Jimmys. A Randall is there, Bobby or Cool or Avila, I can't remember. We all drink quarts of Old Style, except for the Kid, his ma and dad are from Ireland so he'll only drink Mickey's Big Mouth, that's the malt liquor with the shamrock on it, well, 'cause "Mick" I suppose is in the name, and keep an eye out for sᵷuıʞ, or Deuces, or spɹoʅʎɐꓚ, or cops. It's early summer. It's a pain in the ass, but hey, that's when all the good stuff goes down. It's not too hot yet, but the schools have been out for a couple of weeks. That's when it's time to find a car, get packin', head up to Humboldt Park or down to Diversey Avenue to move on some Unknowns. I hate those motherfuckers. Mostly because they're like us, I suppose. You can never tell what they are until the last minute because they're mixed. You know they're gangbangers, but they're all colors. You have to see their shoes (black hi-top Chucks with black laces) or just fuckin' call them out. And that can be a pain in the ass when you're in the Jewel's or the Dominick's with your old man and your shithead brother shopping for everything generic because your dad couldn't make the trade for that brick of gold commod cheese and you have to eat that other crap which, yeah, ew, no, and yeah, they were in my old neighborhood and my brother this one time, well, okay, my brother had to go to school in our neighborhood. It was super sweet, jokes. The school is all Eagles and suʌouʞun. I get home from school after it's been in for about a week and my brother is home.

Why the fuck are you home? I say.

He goes, I'm suspended.

For what? I say.

Beating the shit out of two suʌouʞun, he says.

Well, fuck, I say. The old man is gonna kill you.

Self-defense, he says. He'll get it.

I worry for him a little. I've never seen the old man light into my brother. I've never had to see him make that face with him. Like how when you're taking a beating, and since you can't look the old man in the face, you feel so ashamed for him you look past him, to a spot somewhere on the wall, to a point somewhere in the future where you envision yourself not beating your own son, and you're saying, Thank you, Dad, thank you for showing me how to be a better dad (because it's not like a mom beating; moms beat you because they love you and they can. Dads beat you because they can't). That face, you know?

What happened? I say.

He tells me that these suʍouʜun been fucking with him since the first day of school, talking shit, saying we know your brother is a Royal, we gon' beat your ass, boy. He says, like he always did to whoever, whenever, Fuck you. They say, It's comin', foo. He tells me, Haha, yeah, fuck all that.

So he goes to the boy's room that morning, goes in the stall, and shuts the door but doesn't lock it. Pretty soon these two UKs stroll in talking shit. They head over to the stall, talking 'bout here come that ass beatin' and all, my brother he say come get it, and they open the door and *plow* he hits the first one in the mouth with a dumbbell bar, laughs, and brings it down *crack* on the other one's head. Knocked his ass out, too, he says. Hahahaha, we laugh. Shiiiiit, he says. There was like four teeth on the floor, he says, so I kicked 'em behind the toilet into a puddle of piss. I laugh and say, you should've made a necklace. Damn, he says. Next time, iniiiit?

I think to myself, Shiiiiit. I'm glad I ain't have to go to that shithole school. Y'all can have that. But my brother, dang. He *has* to go. He's only thirteen and this is eighth grade. He can't drop out for three years. And now he's bugging me to get initiated in. He bugs me like every day. I say no every damn time because I don't want my brother gangbanging. If he gets into the set, becomes official, they'll kill him for sure. Thirteen is a shitty age.

My mom kicked me out of the house when I was thirteen, and

my brother came along a year or two later. Remember Kid, the one with the Mickey's Big Mouth? Yeah. He died, shot in the head, and I had to go to his wake and his funeral and all, and my mom was like, You need to be out of this house by the time I get home. I say, Uh, yeah, I'm thirteen. Also, I have to go to this funeral.

Okay, well after that you have to go.

Where? I say.

Go live with your father, she says. I can't have you living in my house with a gun and all the other shit you do.

What? I say.

Get out, she says.

Wow, I say. Fuck you, I guess.

Me and the old man lived in Boys Town at Aldine and Broadway. Kind of near Wrigley Field, but still a haul. I had to take the El a lot, like to school and up to Rogers Park. Or I could take the bus, the Broadway bus. The bus was cool, this older lady pretty hot used to hit on me and give me books to read, and these older uncle dudes would get on pretty regular at Buena. They were big Lakota guys. Hey little brother, they would say, whatcha readin' now? while we sat in the back and they would laugh into their hoodies and talk shit and be loud and hold on tight to their big lunch buckets on their way to work. They had big glasses like me, and crappy skin, ditto, and would say "later" when they got off further down the line and head-up nod, not head-down nod like everyone else. When they stopped getting on the bus, I went back to taking the El.

It kind of sucked to take the El, and I had decisions to make. I could get on at Belmont, but that meant PR Stones, and sometimes suṁouᶍun. Also, it seemed farther from my house even though it probably wasn't. And I would get hit on by creepy old guys more going that way. John Wayne Gacy grabbed up dudes in my neighborhood. Not cool. But it was an all-stops station. So that was good. Still, I always wished I had a gun, preferably a .45, like the one Goof got tattooed on his arm when he was in jail. Do you know that motherfucker got hisself throwed back in jail so he could get one on the other arm to match and to get some of those Calvin Klein jeans he liked? Seriously. And I mean I like a .45 and all, much more than a 9-millimeter, yeah, but still. What the fuck?

I could get on at Addison, and that was all Latin Eagles, and it was before we were supposed to be in the nation with them but never really were because fuck those Eagles, but it was just a B stop so not great, but still you could sneak on there if you were quick like. It wasn't too bad in the morning (but really sucked at night) depending on the time. LeMoyne schoolyard was on the way but set back a bit from Addison, so if you didn't get recognized it was okay, but with all this long hair that was a long shot. Getting off there at night was a worse kind of gamble, though, if the set was mobbed up in the schoolyard, 'cause all the cops were working down the block at Wrigley Field. Mostly it was okay if you could get into the alleyway and just truck along. That seems like it wouldn't make sense and that you should stick to the main street, but nah. One night I got off the El at Addison on a Thursday night around ten and I watched this dude duct tape a half stick of dynamite to a window in a basement apartment and light that shit on fire right on Addison Avenue. I was like, Damn, these sǝup are crazy. So yeah, but if you could quick get to the alley between Wilton and Fremont then head down the alleyway to Cornelia down to Elaine Place and over to Roscoe and out onto Broadway without getting your face smashed in, you were home free. On your way to smoking a little weed and watching *Taxi*, or the *Dukes of Hazzard* if it was a Friday, or reading *The Shining* and scaring the shit out of yourself in different ways entirely and wishing there was some goddamn food in this place.

After I first got the boot, I lived with the old man in the Hawthorne Terrace hotel. A kitchen, a bathroom, a living room where he slept on the couch and I slept in a Murphy bed. What a shithole. But the old man, he likes it so much we move into another place just like it, this time that apartment, that site of all that teenage angst and hunger and lonely, that was at 549 West Aldine. One morning he's going to work and he says to me, Speedy, check the roach motels and see if you need to move them. We had these seriously needed Raid® roach motel things in the apartment. They were little boxes lined with glue and you put them along the wall. Roaches check in but they don't check out I think is how the commercial went.

He leaves for work, I have my coffee and a cigarette, get ready for school, and check the roach motel. I have to do a double take. Sonofabitch, there's a fucking mouse in there. Shit. I'm holding it and looking at this mouse looking at me and back and forth to the leg it's trying to chew off so it can get checked the fuck out of this crappy motel. Damnit, I don't know what to do with it. I don't want it to get away, but I don't have like a weight or anything to drop on its head, and I would never do that to a book, so I'm like fuck what do I do, so I put a big pan of water on the stove and I keep shaking the mouse in the trap so he can't get a good grip on that leg of his, and when the water finally boils I just kind of slow slide him into the pan and that's that for him and the trap. When the old man finally comes home he's already laughing. Did you move the trap? he says, drunk as shit. Hahaha, I say. Yeah. We have to get a new one, I say. I tell him the story about the pan of ignoble demise. He laughs and laughs. He says, Shiiiiit. I laid there this morning listening to that li'l fucker going to town underneath the newspaper pile, and then he just stopped for a minute, and then I could see that box jumping around. Shit, I say, I got to get Speedy to move that trap. He'll get a kick out of it. We laugh and he says, Jeet? I say, No. Jew? He says, No, squeet, like we sometimes do, so we head down to the diner and it's a Francheezie for me. Fuckin' A good. Life is so fuckin' good sometimes.

So this building on Aldine. It used to be a nice hotel way back in the day, then it was an SRO, and then apartments, so we live in this little studio for a bit, same shit, Murphy bed, cucarachas, mice, but what's good? When you have mice, you have no roaches, so take your pick. Then my brother gets the boot too, and he shows up, and we move down the hall. To a one bedroom apartment. We jam three beds into the bedroom and have a combination living room / dining room / kitchen, plenty of room for the old man to break those dishes. We're on the third floor, so we have a view. Of Broadway. And the gangway across the street, where transvestite hookers take care of business, day, night, and day. Also, the pigeons on the roof. Tons of pigeons. I have a wristrocket. That's a slingshot made of aluminum and rubber tubing, but with an extension at the bottom so it braces against your wrist, and the velocities you can get are stunning, really.

We're bored one day in the summer, and we don't have any money to take the El, and even though you could sneak on at Addison where someone had cut away the grate from where the back porch of this apartment met the El platform, some Eagles had taken over that whole building so that shit was out, and we had just walked up to the old neighborhood twice that week and that'll wear you out, I don't care how much energy you got, because that haul is like about four hours long and you have to do it along the lake and not down Clark or Broadway because it's mostly sƃuᴉʞ and spɹoʅʎɐꓭ that whole way, and who needs that shit unless you're packing and we weren't, so we just stay home that day and smoke cigarette butts out of the ashtrays and two roaches I had been saving, and then my brother is like,

Hey, lemme see that wristrocket. I got some ball bearings.

Cool, I say, and

we spend about a half hour shooting pigeons, trying our best to catch them on the wing and drop them dead onto Broadway. We hit one on the roof at 560 West across the street but can't hit jack over Broadway and probably send twenty pounds of ball bearings into various alleyways and businesses and the church a block over. We fuck around, talk shit, but not a whole lot. My brother is about as talkative as the old man, which means he's good for a half dozen doublets a day, and four of those sentences will be either "Give me a cigarette" or "Go fuck yourself." I'm used to that, so the ten or so full sentences he's offered up today are unusual at least if not actually moving over into unsettling. This can't last, I think.

My brother has these heavy eyebrows. They meet in the middle of his face over these deep-set eyes, and he's light and he looks like Rasputin, and I always think that right between those eyes where you can barely even see there's a button labeled "self-destruct" and he pushes it every couple of days and then sometimes he just pushes it so hard it sticks, and then he gets warrants and has to take states off his list of wonderful places he'd like to, but never can, visit again. I could see his finger inching over that way.

He looks at me for a second and laughs and then sends a ball bearing out the window and across the street toward a window in a third-floor apartment where it sails so fast it just ploops through the glass and doesn't even break anything.

Holy shit.

That was cool.

Lemme see.

Fuck you.

Lemme try.

Okay. Here.

I take the wristrocket, grab one of those smooth chrome pieces of shot, and I aim and I pull back, way back, and let go, and damn.

It just fuckin' sails right through the glass in the upper corner of the window. Hahaha. Damn.

That *is* cool.

I think, I'm going to remember this moment.

See Dad? it's not all bad.

And you know it's not all bad 'cause that same dad, that laying on of the hands dad, one night you're all (well, okay, kinda) grown up and you're at that dad's place and you're drinking and your infant daughter is in the other room sleeping like a . . . baby, and your woman, your wife, your best friend, your She Who Puts Up with All This Shit, sleeps the sleep of the just and that roll-eyed, vodka-steamed-from-nostrils, pressed-lipped, dark-faced vortex of anger and fury says, Aaaah, I know I was a shitty dad. I could never do the things you do, man. I'm really proud of you.

I suppose I shouldn't expect a whole lot more. Dad had one book—Plato's *Republic*—and two rules. Don't get arrested. I'm not coming to get you. And don't ever cheat on your woman. If you're done, move on.

How's that for guidance, for life rules, for structure, for love, and for warmth?

Eventually we pack up that book, and my books, some my brother had, what was left of the dishes, the beds, and the TV, and we move across the street. It takes us about an hour to move. I liked that. When I got older, moving day meant filling up a couple of hefty bags and calling a cab.

One day me and the brother, we're sitting in the dining room of that new apartment. Smoking cigarettes, drinking coffee, hating the new Rolling Stones single that the sad-ass DJ on the Loop played back to back, watching the snow come down outside, and I say, Manwhatthefuck, why is it so fuckin' cold in here all the time? We have a fuckin' radiator and shit (which the old man placed TV dinner trays of water on so we could have a humidifier). I'm freezing my nuts off.

He takes a drag off the Old Gold filter from a pack we had gone in on that I wrote the note for, and he points a finger up toward the curtain. I look at his squinty eyebrows on that already closed and shut down face, his eyes almost invisible, but I follow his line of sight, and he says, Lookit that shit—wind blowing right through. We pull back the sheet that's hanging there and look, hahahaha, there's like six or eight gumball-size holes in the thick frosted glass and the cold air is just pouring right through.

I'm outside the library and I go to call Choochie at the payphone by the Adelphi Theater on Clark and Estes. Fridays are new movies. I'm remembering the look in Hector's eyes last night right before Choochie smashed him in the face with the butt end of a fire extinguisher as he came running after us in the gangway off the alley by the Naugles (worstfoodever) and how he made this weird noise as he was falling to the ground and then he didn't make any noise at all. I put in twenty cents and it rings just once.

James, I say when he picks up.

Hey, Teddy.

What movie is playing tonight?

What?

What's the new movie this week?

I don't know.

Well look up. You're standing right there, I say.

Who cares, he says.

You do. You said we were all going this week because Taco and them were gonna try and make a move on the theater.

Well fuck it, yeah. We'll just go then. We'll be here.

Yeah, fine. But what's the movie?

Who gives a shit?

I do, I say.

I don't, he says.

What's the fucking movie?

Fuck you, Teddy, he says.

I'm like, What, man?

Fuck you.

What's your problem, James?

Fuck you, he says. You know I can't read.

Shit.

Choochie can't read.

It's like a flashback reel. All those fuckin' times I'm remembering now, all this time, Choochie couldn't read. How much is that, James? What's it say? What stop do we get off at?—look at the map. How come you dropped out in eighth grade? How do you go through life like that? How angry, how frustrated would you be? Every kick to Carla's face. Every punch to a peewee's stomach. Every look over every sight and hammer. That stare looks back at everyone who ever failed him, who never knew him, who ever betrayed him.

Like pain; pain at reading a story in the newspaper. And then later on thinking, Man, that pain didn't end when people stopped reading the article, that's for sure. I wonder where that pain is now. Not too often, but yeah. Whenever I stand too long in front of a theater.

Whenever I look up to read what's playing tonight.

IDIOT

I had a friend named Idiot. One day I strangled him. Well, not to death, but close enough. That fucking guy. He was a relentless torment. Twice my size, wicked, and ceaseless. I just couldn't do it anymore, couldn't take his shit.

I watched his face change colors, blue to green, watched as tiny red flares appeared in the whites of his eyes, capillaries or whatever getting blown out. Like the swirl of a food-coloring drop in a coffee cup of vinegar at Easter, or when you've been drinking milk and you spit in the toilet. My face so close, jaw clenched so hard, drool slipping between the cracks in my teeth and onto his face. No sound escaped his lips. I wondered what kind of sound he would make if he could make a sound. Would it be like you imagined mimes would sound if they could talk? I always thought mimes would sound like Christmas carolers if they could talk, and that's why they didn't. Because no one would let them.

He started to make sounds up in his nasal cavities, so I pressed harder, my thumbnails bright white at his larynx. Still, he was smiling. Motherfucker.

Idiot. Ids. Smart but not too smart. Ids who took a hockey puck to the nuts. Fell out of trees. Whose head bounced on more sidewalks than all of us put together. Ids who had the first big tattoo out of all of us. It was on his arm (we all had tattoos on our hands, but the one on the arm seemed like a bigger deal). Guess what it said. Yeah. "IDS."

Yeah. Ids.

Ids was my buddy, my pal, my boy, my best friend. I used to spend the night at his house all the time because my house sucked. That worked out. He always had food, too, so bonus there. And he had a stepdad who was a total asshole, which was horrible, but on the flip his stepdad looked like Gomez Addams but with a huge Tom Selleck moustache, and that was hilarious, so things got balanced out, in a way. Plus, that guy was a drinker. Yeah. Booze everywhere.

Ids's mom? She was awesome. And hot. And redheaded. Smoked all kinds of weed. And after she divorced Gomez, she let people party at the house. But not me. I guess I'd always have some weird place there for her, maybe because she knew me from the time I was pretty little. Fine. Whatever. Oh yeah. Hahahaha. And they had a dog—if you'd even call it that—a Maltese named "Mr. Dickens." Hahaha. Shiiiiiiit.

In addition to that dog a lot of people hung out at the house. People who were selling weed and whatnot for her, and tic for her sister when she came home from the army. One of the guys who hung around a lot was called Turf. I don't know if it was because he rode Turf from over by Senn H. S. or because that was his name. Turf looked like Phil Lynott from Thin Lizzy. Even had the same moustache. Except he talked like Tommy Chong. It was really unsettling. And I don't know if it was because that was his voice, or because he was fucked up *all* the time, or a combination thereof, but yeah, I hated having to hear him talk. Good thing he was the quiet type. What I didn't know was that, like more than a couple of the guys, he hit his girlfriend. I never understood that shit at all. Dudes had some fuckin' problems. Not cool. So this one time Turf beat up Janay and got his own ass beat for it. Janay ended up with what I suppose was her protector. That shit seemed a little medieval to me, but she was happy, and that's what counts in the end, I guess.

The guy who put an end to Turf's reign of terror—and I guess an end to Turf in general because, come to think of it, I never saw him again—was a guy named Max. Max who looked like Karl I was in the navy with except where Max liked George Benson and had a good soul and had spent time in the joint and respected people, Alabama Karl was a one-man lynch mob in his little pea brain, spent his time working out, quietly admired his Iowa workout buddy's body, and low-key intimidated country folks on the mess deck. What a piece of shit. I can still see him sitting across and down from me at chow, that lower lip stuck out with chew, upper lip dusted with a blonde pedostache, pouring syrup on his grits and yuckyuckyucking it up with that fucking Foghorn Leghorn accent, which by itself is just fine, but filtered through his cracker-ass adenoidal rage just made you want to go out and burn down a trailer.

Max was a good dude. Quiet in the way that people who have seen way too much shit are quiet, and thoughtful, and appreciatively kind in ways that most people never are or ever will be. He'd literally give you his last nickel, or the shirt off his back, all the while owning the ability to take those very things from you if the thought crossed his mind while you passed a joint back and forth, and the look you'd occasionally see on his face made you think he was at least thinking about exercising that skill just for the fun of it.

Those older guys, those Grease and CJOs, Royals and Popes who had done time, those were probably some of the best people I've ever known in my life, even now. Generous, thoughtful, always looking out for other people. If there's an underappreciated group of folks just trying to make it all work, it's them.

That trying to keep it together, make sense of it all, that takes a daily *want*. Something you need to renew. It has to be a hum in the back of your head, or a tiny blue light out in front, like one those deep-sea angler fish have; you self-illuminate and keep that prize in front of your own eyes. For sure there's a certain level of desire that gets met where it's kind of like reading *Justine* and *then* reading *The 120 Days of Sodom*, that forbiddenness, that sense of oh, man, I shouldn't be reading this that you want so bad and it bubbles right out of and crusts on over from *Blood Meridian* so good that if you start with that piece but read out of turn, say, *Child of God, The Road*, and *No Country for Old Men*, by the time you're at *Suttree* you're just all shut up already, and head on down the road with your big man misogynist fantasies, and please don't stop in Hollywood to make a movie all so disappointing like that cookie you grab at your friend's house and you're all, yeah, kickass, but then you take a bite and chew and these are fucking *raisins*, low-light impostor chocolate chips, and that's why you never really eat at other people's houses if you can help it, because they all make shit wrong, put mushrooms in chili like some kind of fucking hippies. But this is different, this is you wanting, knowing that this is like listening to Amebix, or the first time you heard Venom after seeing the Black Metal cover—shit, that will change your life in the best of evil ways, not like watching *The Exorcist* in the theater, seeing the big X rating on the giant green screen, being so fucking scared every night for six months that you run and jump from the edge of the doorway onto the mattress so . . . *she* doesn't get you. Fuck. That. That's different. And that's not this. This is one of those moments you only get so many of in life, it's . . . discovery, in the end. Not only of the thing itself, this forbidden sort of arcane knowledge, exquisite in its presence in your young, so-much-ahead-of-you life that it has room to grow and occupy a space in your spirit in a meaningful way, a way probably not available anymore in a world of all things so digitally available, but of the want that comes with the thing, the serpent's apple that promises all the things you'll forget you wanted if you're not careful, if you don't tend the garden of your soul. This is when you decide this neighborhood is not going to be your cemetery too. And you know you have to leave.

But the options are limited. And luck is even harder to come by. Maybe you look at life in a certain way, and maybe the backlight, the illumination that comes through in the eyes you use to look at your world, as narrow and fucked up as it may be, maybe that light gets picked up by someone who, for some never to be known reason or another, just happens to catch it one day, one right day, one fortuitous day, and decides that maybe your life should and could be different. Maybe they say you're too smart for this shit, but you're a big pain in our ass, and maybe if you stay you'll end up doing three to five in Joliet, or you'll do four in the service, depending on the decision you give me right here right now.

You're not sure how this has happened, how you've come to the point where you've got no more than 2point5 seconds to decide which way your life is about to go. They tell you how *they* think you got there, whether it jives with your story or not. This is what they say, Lenny and Squiggy, those fuckers:

Well, you know how you and a bunch of other Royals decided to have that big party the other night, a week or so ago?

No.

Yeah. So that big party. Drinking, getting high, all that good shit you like to do . . .

Fuck, I think. I knew it. Son of a bitch.

And that's one thing, but when you take a can of black spray paint and tag the dad's bedroom, well, we gotta come find you. That was too easy. What the fuck were you thinking?

Fucking Frankie. That dipshit. I remember him coming out of the bedroom. Hey, Teddy. You should come check it out.

Anyway, we got a call there, Injun. Had to go investigate.

This was the crib we went to, Stacey saying over and over you should come party at my place. Me asking, Where's your dad? and her saying, Oh, he's in Jamaica. I should've known. Who the fuck can afford to go to Jamaica in January?

And when we get there, Teddy, it's the funniest thing. We toss the place, make like we're gonna print it and whatnot, but hey, what the fuck, we find a shit ton of junk—brown not white, but whatever. A bunch of weed. And some sawed-offs and a couple nice pistols. Nines, you know? None of that .38 caliber bullshitcheapshit.

Fuck. That shit ain't mine, I say.

Well, we know that, Midget. You're the smartest guy we know. There's no way you would leave that shit behind.

You're goddamn right, I say.

But you know what? You know whose shit it is, Teddy?

Whose?

Ah. This is the best part. The guy's an ASA. An assistant state's attorney.

I know what it means.

We know you do. We just wanted to say it out loud. And watch your face when we did.

Motherfucker.

Nah. The only one getting fucked around here is you. They do fake war whoops at me with their fat, sweaty hands.

What's that supposed to mean?

Well, that shit now belongs to you, not to the ASA, who needs a lesson in how to hide his habit a little better. Which makes me think, How the fuck did *you* not see it? Were you fucking the girl?

No, man. Ew. Shit. Give me some credit.

86

Well, anyway. You blew it.

I was in the other room with that Gonzalez chick. I wasn't anywhere near any of that shit.

We know. Fuck. It was like a gangbanger Christmas in there. Two sawed-off Mossberg 12-gauges. A Glock. An H&K. Hilarious. We could tell you didn't touch the spray paint, either. You better give Frankie some lessons. And tell him to fuckin' pay attention.

Goddamnit.

Anyway, this is our big chance to get rid of you. We can't have you stay in the neighborhood. You're too smart. You get away with too much shit. We can't really keep up, and since we don't have to, well, yeah. You gotta go. This right here will net you a long stretch. Three to five at least. You can do those downstate, Joliet. Or four in the service. It's up to you.

What's it gonna be? they ask.

Fuck me, I say.

Yup. Hahahaha, they go. Happy seventeenth birthday, shithead, they say.

I still don't really celebrate my birthday.

What's it gonna be? they wanna know.

Anchors aweigh, fuckers.

Hahaha.

Yeah. Fuck you.

Hey. Careful, they say. We weren't worried, though, they say. Yeah. Goof said he'd take the rap anyway. Enjoy your haircut, Geronimo. We'll keep an eye on your ma.

Lenny takes a fake swing at me.

Squiggy sort of scratches his balls, or whatever he's got going on down there, and grins, pops a pink bubble from the gum he's always chewing, eyes dead and unseen behind his aviators.

I light a smoke and tell myself stories that I hope will keep me sane.

And Ids? What about Ids? you want to know. I let him go after I made him promise to stop fucking with me. And he kept that promise. I had to throw trump on his ass. I told him, Look, motherfucker, you know I'm smarter than you. I'm half your size but twice your brain. I'll come after you. I'll use everything I've got up there. You'll be dead and people will wring their hands, and preachers will preach, and mothers will lament, and girlfriends will cry, but you'll be gone. And I'll make that happen.

You know it's true.

Yeah, he said, Teddy. I know.

The light in my eye told him I knew he knew.

And I never blinked.

BLOOD ON THE TRACKS/ NO MAS

Summer meant a lot of different things, but mostly it meant we listened to George Benson so we could imagine ourselves on Broadway and smoked the sweetleaf listening to Black Sabbath and figured out what the Sugarhill Gang was trying to tell us while we hung out in the park, our park, Pottawattomie Park, the one next to the tracks, *those* tracks, the Chicago and Northwestern tracks, not the El tracks. It was cool that we could pick our own tunes, and cool, too, when we could fight about it. Nothing like a ass-whuppin', because fuck Led Zeppelin, to break up a hot, sleepy afternoon. The arrival of the boombox was a welcome jump in the quality of summertime soundtracks, and it brought a semblance of control to a lot of otherwise unruly lives (when you weren't worried about wasting batteries on rewinds) and was a touch or two better than the Super CFL of those childhood nights where I wondered about what went on Behind Closed Doors and what was wrong with Angie Baby and was Billy a Hero in Viet Nam or in the Westerns I always watched my old man watch, and why should Sundown Beware and all that other creepy shit that came on the air through my tiny, tinny, single-earplugged crystal radio that only played in mono anyways so who cared until the O'Jays or the Spinners finally came on. We hung together strong all day long and drank and smoked and listened to tunes and talked shit and beat each other's asses. But there were times when all that was a lot, and I'd sit on the guardrail next to the street across from this weird hippy community–type garden they kept planting and we kept stealing from. Some days there would be carrots, but some days we'd have to go try and get apples and wild grapes from the grounds of this Catholic girl's school—behabited lunatics from the in-house nunnery would chase us away with what everyone said was a German shepherd whose teeth the good sisters had had removed but none of us wanted to find out, and I would try to imagine my life burning across the sky. But when I put my dreams on that horizon, no matter how dark it got, they pulsed like a daytime comet, as if I held hands with Kohoutek that one summer, embraced that fizzled and fuzzy, barely visible streak, our ill-formed tail flashing for one sad moment, passing not like Bruce Lee would in July but more like James Garner and that camel in *One Little Indian*.

One day the stepmother offered to give me a ride up north (the old man got remarried, and I want to say, Well, that's a whole nother story for another time, but it's not. It's just a second marriage. Yawn, and shit.) and I was like daaaaang. She never does that. I'ma take that ride and

so I did. We headed up north. I can't remember why she was going there. Maybe to look for a new apartment or something. We were all living in this kinda too-small place on Aldine that was surprisingly drafty in the winter and, well, yeah. It was time to move anyway. Prolly was going to kill the old man to go more than a couple of blocks, though. I always thought to myself, Hey, weren't we nomads, some of the most mobile people of the Plains, but here's my dad like a fucking Creek corn planter or something. He never went anywhere if he could help it. Or maybe it was a routine thing. Because if the bar was ten miles away, he'd figure out how to get there, no lie.

Anyways, I hop in the car with the stepmom. She asks some perfunctory stepmomish questions of her teenage stepson, and then we smokesmokesmoke all the way up Lake Shore Drive and I just loooook out the window. Man. I love Lake Shore Drive when there's no traffic, and that was a stunningly beautiful, sunny, traffic-free, light off the lake, beautiful blue aquaclear day, one of the two or three you get every year in Chicago whether you want them or not, and you can't help but be thankful you're alive to see them.

I flash forward a couple of years. I'm in Beirut. In the navy. There's this Hook on the boat, too. He's a CVL. His name is Aldo— this West Side motherfucker, a vice lord from way the fuck out there, like a Central Avenue or Cicero Insane or Conservative Vic or some shit. He got in my face one day when we were in the chow line, like wassup Folks? (Tattoos back then were a far rarer thing, much more noticeable, especially on the hands, and when you're a fan of the explicit, well, there's no hiding who you are.) And I'm like, Man, fuck you, we in Beirut, we ain't got time for this shit, and he kept on talking, so I clanged him in the face with my tray and then held the metal edge of that tray up to his neck, and these country boys from Arkansas or some shit were like, Whoa, what the fuck y'all doin', we got to get along here, and I laughed even though we ain't heard of Rodney King yet, and I said, Yeah, truce I guess, and he said, Yeah, but I'm payin' you back when this shit is over, and I said, Deal, and then we talked all where y'all from what's your set and all that, and I was like, Hey, I went to school with Lord Black and we made fun of Borroso that M/H bitch, and he was like, Alright, and we was all good for a long time. One day Aldo says to me,

Hey, folks, check it out. Looks like the South Side out there on the beach,
    and
    I said, Yeah, it does.
    And it did. Me and him are standing there on the catwalk, boat in Beirut harbor, sun setting, magic light coming down like when you're in bed and its summer and you have just a sheet and you fluff it out with your feet and it comes down light and cool and it's like that and I'm saying,
    Hey, this is alright,
    even if I am standing here watching with this fucking vice lord, and then wink
    wink
    tiny red stars flash from one of the buildings, about eight floors up,
    and then the crash rolls out over the water at us,
    the sound of two explosions just hitting our ears as two spots on the facing building
    light up
    and I watch the bricks fall
    and the flame lick out up the wall,
    and I think back to the Taylor Homes
    that are now gone but not forgotten,
    and I'm glad I can't hear anyone scream.
    At either place.

The stepmom drops me off near the park, and I head over to Jimmy's. It was early in the afternoon. Or late in the morning. But it was summer, and it was one of those days. I figured I'd stop by, see what was up. Go steal a bottle of wine or something. OP had these new weird bottles of flavored wine. But not like MD 20/20 grape or banana or whatever, these were Piña Colada / Strawberry

Daiquiri / Tequila Sunrise—shit like that. I thought maybe steal a bottle or two of that and a bunch of disposable lighters that we could throw in a paper bag and light on fire (apparently I was still reeling from cosmic disappointment stemming from that fraud of a comet and felt the need to light up the sky on my own) and kick it at the park for a while. But no one was home. I laid on the bell for a minute straight, long enough to hear the dog bark. Jimmy's family had the only real dog out of anyone we knew, and it was a serious asshole-mean German shepherd named Sheba. You couldn't turn your back on the dog or it would bite you. Hard. Still, nothing. I sat on the stoop to wait. Pulled my last Kool out of my sock and lit it up.

Pretty soon Jimmy's little sister comes walking up, swearing and tearing.

What's up? I say.

Shit, she says. It fuckin' took forever to get home.

Where were you?

Downtown. I wanted to do some shopping early (that meant shop*lifting*, but I don't quibble).

So. What happened?

Man, she says. I got stuck on the train for like an hour right before we got to Jarvis. Some dumbass got electrocuted on the third rail.

Dang, I say. That sucks.

Yeah, she says. They had to pry him off there, so that took a while. Then they had to clean it up.

I shudder a little.

Anyway, she says, pulling out her keys, come on up.

Okay, I say.

We head upstairs. Their hallway always smelled weird. Not like the apartment hallways over on Devon past Western smelled though.

Those hallways. Man. I hated that fucking smell. I never knew what it was until years later. It was curry. Jeezuschrist. I mean, yeah, I like to eat it every now and again, but the concentrated smell. Man.

But it's okay, because that smell I never really learned to put up with was the prelude to this job I would get. The reason I was in those hallways was because I had a gig handing out flyers for Danny's Pizza on Clark Street. Danny's, which was by Luigi's, which was by Alberto's . . . that little stretch of Clark Street was awesome. There was a pizza place and two bars on just about every corner, and we had the Affy Tapple place. Broken stick caramel apples for a nickel. That's my old-man moment.

Anyway, I was putting these flyers in apartment lobbies and hallways all over the neighborhood. The flyer was a menu that doubled as a coupon. I think one side said "Free quart of RC with your order!" or something like that. Actually, I'm pretty sure it did, because every single pizza place in the neighborhood gave you a free quart of RC with your delivery . . .

Okay. I'm putting these flyers in people's hallways and doors and mailboxes and everywhere they could go. I'm working, "Because that's what you do"—Ted Sr. This job is way better than the last one I had—these guys had this business out in the suburbs and they would come pick us up in the city to hang coupon bags on suburban house doors and avoid their denizen's dogs and glares on super-early Saturday mornings. This restaurant gig was cool, way better than that suburban shit, and I'm not gonna lie, I was digging the food we'd get every now and again, and it was in the afternoon and it was late fall and, man, there's not much better for walking and thinking than late afternoon in a North Side Chicago neighborhood in October/November when the deep cold's not there yet and the light is always 4:45; always Magic Light, always Anything Is Possible Light, and you have your bullshit school day behind you and all that you can imagine in front of you and no one looks at you and no one cares what you do and it doesn't get freer than that and you get paid, besides? That's good shit right there.

The bonus comes after I've been working there for a while. I'm watching what's happening. I see cool things, like this kid from my grammar school's parents would come in every Wednesday because Wednesday was All You Can Eat Spaghetti Night, complete with lots of loafer cops. I had never seen this kid's parents before, I think the kid's name was Terry, but you know I'm probably saying that because he was a ginger, but not like Muck that redheaded fuck. Terry, we'll say, because that seems like an Irish name, was this quiet kid from school, one of those nondescript kids you look at and you can't really remember what they look like but that's why you remember what they look like, and their faces are a little bit shiny and they seem to be not yet formed—when you try to remember what they look like it's kind of from the side and there's an eye but no real defined *form* to their face and it's unsettling, but not horrible, and yeah, he was one of those kids.

So he brings in his mom and dad, and I see he's sort of leading them in, and it's dark in Danny's all the time so sure, whatever, but then I'm like, Oh, he's kind of walking them over, which is kind of weird because now I notice that they're both blind, and I think, Shit, they're probably better off than he is since it's so dark in here, and I'm like, Okay, back to work making up these flyer packets so I can head out on the job, but about twenty minutes later Don calls my name. Yeah. "Don." The owner was named Don. And he had these big '70s glasses that were a little bit amber tinted and these big-collared patterned silk shirts and he drank coffee out of those tiny cups. Coffee. Not espresso. Shit. It was the '70s. I had never even heard of espresso, but between you and me now, yeah—he was drinking coffee out of those tiny cups, tryna front like. And he smoked cigarettes one right after the other. Not chain-smoked like when you light one right off the butt of the other, but long enough to crack his knuckles and look around the restaurant from his table, centered in the aisle between the booths right off the kitchen, and admire all that he had built. He calls out my name and I hustle over from one of the booths.

Teddy,

can you get me a coffee? he says.

Sure, Don, I say.

I bring him his coffee from one of the big percolators we got in the kitchen.

Have a seat, he says.

I sit.

Smoke? he says.

Sure, I say.

You been working here for a while, huh? he says, shaking a pack of Tareytons at me.

Yup, I say, take one out, side-eye look at the weird filter.

You wanna learn how to cook? he says (the "k" at the end has like a glottal stop).

Sure, I say.

You start when you get back from doing those flyers, he says.

Sure, I say, put the square in my mouth, and light it.

Hold on, he says. I'll be right back.

He picks up this envelope he's been tapping on the side of that little coffee cup of his and walks over to one of the booths near the front. I turn around in my chair and my eyes are following his tall, narrow ass walking across the restaurant, moving slow like in their sockets. They stop when they see Terry's parents enjoying All You Can Eat Spaghetti Night because, well, okay, they're putting the Parmesan on their spaghettis and they're using their hands to sense the heat that rises from the plate so they know where and when to stop with the cheese, and I think, Man, that is the coolest shit right there, and then Don pulls up at the booth crossways from theirs and sits down. Across from this old Irish fuck beat cop sergeant type with a ton of face who I thought never left the community policing office, who is eating and sweating and still wearing that checkerboard-banded hat, his mug red and constantly in motion.

I take a drag off my cigarette and watch through the slowly blowing smoke in front of my face. Don and the cop talk for a minute, exchanging what are surely bullshit pleasantries, and then Don slides that plain-white letter-size envelope over toward that fat red hand. Loud laughter erupts out of the fatter redder face while gnarly hand and freshly greased envelope disappear inside cop leather, the flag of Chicago briefly oblique as chubby arm and shoulder lift to accommodate the proceeds from his unearned payday. They chitchat a bit more, probably about how it must be getting pretty cold up there yukyukyuk in the apartment above the restaurant for the twelve or so Mexicans that live there and keep an eye on the bread deliveries and make pizzas and do whatever else Don wants, but probably not, probably talking about where Sergeant O'Slaughter is going for vacation now, or something else entirely, you know, like disco or civil rights. Hahaha.

Don comes back to the table. I put out my smoke in the ashtray. A tiny bit of the cherry burns into the side of my finger, but I don't say nothin'. I think Don sees it, or else he just smiles like that for no reason—either way, I don't know which is worse.

Pays $2.50 an hour, cash. Work from 4:00 til close, he says.

We close at 2:00 a.m., right? I say.

Yup, he says.

Well, shit. I don't think I can do it, I say.

Why not? he says.

Curfew, I say.

Curfew? What the fuck is that? he says.

It's the law, I say. 10:30 on weeknights, 11:30 on the weekends. Everyone under seventeen has to be off the streets.

Hahahahaha. He laughs. Curfew, he says.

There ain't no curfew, Don says.

You work for *us*, he says.

I smile to myself and say, *Yeah I do.*

Bonus. I learn how to cook my ass off in this place. I make cole-
slaw by hand, pizzas, pastas, all kinds of shit in big, super-hot
ovens. Subs, slices, baked fuckin' ziti even. All that. And this is
good, because I still do all the cooking in my house to this day. My
old man? He cooked once a week when we were growing up. On
Sunday. Week 1. Chili. 2. Beef stew. 3. Spaghetti. 4. Goulash (maca-
roni and tomatoes). That was it. In a big aluminum pot that will
probably give all of us OldTimer's. And that was what we ate all
week, until it ran out. You want something else?

Make it your fuckin' self.

So I was learning how to make shit at home, but running out of
options. Eggs. Garlic bread in the broiler. You know, generic white
bread with margarine (the old man called it "oleo") and garlic salt.
That was about it. There really wasn't anything else in the house.
The old man was cheap that way. He left money on the counter
one time for me to buy milk. Two one-dollar bills. Milk cost $1.75.
'Bout six weeks later he goes,

So you got that quarter?

Fuck.

He gave me a dollar a day when I was going to school. Cost
thirty-five cents each way with a student bus pass. Rolls were six
cents each, and so was a carton of milk. If I wanted lunch I bought
two rolls and a milk. I had twelve cents left over. By Friday I had
sixty cents saved up. You know what that meant:

Please sell my son a package of Old Gold Filters.
Thanks,
Pop

A pack of smokes was fifty-five cents. So I had change. Did candy cost a nickel back then, too, Grandpa? You bet your ass it did. Well, okay, fuckin' SloPokes were a nickel. And Necco Wafers were a dime, if you could wait another Friday. If I couldn't wait, and I smoked too much, then I had to make up the money somewhere. The easiest way to do that was to walk all the way up to the Jarvis El station. It was two stops farther away then the one by my school, but it was mostly our territory, so not too bad. And at Jarvis, if you stuck your back up against the telephone pole in the alley next to the tracks, you could sort of walk up the wall with yourself wedged in between there. Then when you got to the top of the wall, about sixteen feet up at least, you had to make sure no trains were coming, then hophophop onto the tracks and over the third rail and onto the platform and give everybody who saw you do it a dirty look and then just be all nonchalant.

Yeah. I had had about enough of that shit.

So do I want to learn how to cook in this mobbed-up joint where I ain't gotta worry about the local cops and take home about a buck and a quarter a week and buy my own smokes and shit and some pants that fit and some new chucktaylors? You're fuckin' right I do.

And do I learn. Like nobody's business. Years later in the boonies of Northern Maine I make a fuckin' sandwich in my own place for Martha Stewart *before* she went to the joint.

My. That's delicious, she says.

I just smile one of those smiles.

Don would've been proud all the way around.

We get to the apartment. Ria sets her shit down on the counter. I walk into the living room to look around and the dog bites me in the leg. Fuck.

I hate this fucking dog,

this dog Sheba that they cook chicken for. Man. I haven't had a piece of chicken in about eighteen months. Fuck you, dog. I give her the finger. I flick on the stereo. Ria and Jimmy's old man isn't home. It's Saturday, so Papa Louie's at the bar. Their ma, who I call Ma, too, because she insists that I do, so I do and not just because they're Sicilian, is working. She waitresses down the street. I light up a cigarette and glare at the dog. She doesn't like smoke, so I smoke a lot when she's around—it helps to keep the biting down.

Klaus Meine screams at me about his Lovedrive and some winged whore. I ask Ri what happened.

From the kitchen she says,

Some dumbass, I don't know. He just got zapped. And stuck to the rail, right by the station. It took forever to get him off the tracks, I guess. Such a pain in the ass. Damn. Oh well. What's

new with you?

Nothing much, I say.

The dog growls.

Go eat your fuckin' chicken, I say.

What, Teddy? she says.

Nothing, I say.

Where's Jimmy?

I don't know, she says. He was still here when I left, but he said something about going to the movies.

Fuck, I say. Must've went downtown, init? No movies around here until nighttime.

Yeah, probably, she says.

I cut Klaus off mid-yell. I flash back to the day I taught everyone how to sneak on at Jarvis so we could go downtown to watch kung fu movies all day and beat the living shit out of each other all the way home. Like you do.

I give Ri a hug.

She jumps a little, and then hugs me back.

I keep my voice from cracking and I say,

Okay, well, I'll go see who else is around. They won't be home 'til late anyway.

Okay, she says.

See you later, she says.

I shut the door on my way out. The dog never tried to bite me at all.

I walk outside and down to the corner at Fargo and Damen. I look toward the park

and

I see that idiot Freckles walking my way, walking with his ugly girlfriend. I'm sorry. But there's no other way to put it. She was just . . . ugly.

Hey! Teddy! he says.

I just walk away.

I find out later all that happened, how it went down. Some people blamed Freckles, said he pushed him. Others said Jimmy slipped on his way across the tracks. Some said he slipped off the platform.

None of those things matter, really. None of those things can get between the skin of your face and the palm of your hand slammed so tight to your forehead that tries to drive the tears back into your face, the hand that tries to push this staggering disbelief back inside and down where it belongs, a kind of thing you might handle later in life but then it's called grief, and right now that thing is called something else and it's so profound you can't name it and it would be devastatingly tragic if it was the one and only time it ever happened, so instead of sadness it's anger and it's frustration and you know it's not the last and so you mourn for something else entirely, something you might never be able to name but something that will rule your life if you let it out of the box, something that can ruin it if you keep it locked up, but something that will become your rudder if you play it out right.

And then one day after walking away from a nasty shit-talking fight with some of boys, which I won, of course, there I was. I sort of came to and looked around. I was alone, and felt it deeply, but I envisioned myself envisioning this moment, older and tired somewhere, maybe in a shitty suburb, or worse, maybe around the corner from right fucking here, and wishing I had come to that moment differently, and I knew the only way to make a different difference was to re-envision myself. I didn't know then what I needed to do, but I knew this, *all* this, was *fucked*, wasn't for me, would kill me dead if I let it, and I wasn't ready to die just then. Not at that age. Not with that buzz, not with that smile on my face, not with that clear forehead, that long hair, that tanned brown skin, that girlfriend, that ice-cold quart of Old Style, that boombox, that song, that moment of sublime warmth, no soup, no cops, no crap, no fear. No way.

I just smile and think.

This line comes in my head, and it won't let go.

"Much to do," the old man said, "even as a sea of bastards is still bushy about us."

HOUND

I sat in the back of the bus and wished this fucker would stop for a smoke break. I'd been looking out the same goddamned window for three hours. Cactus, rock, hill, sand. Cactus, rock, hill, sand. Cactus, rock, hill, sand. Cactus, rock, hill, sand. Jeezus.

The guy in front of me, Jesus, I think, he's asleep. I need to wake him up, because I need this cat on my side. I get that he's probably tired, given our earlier conversation, but we need to stop.

Jesus.

Como?

Dude. Wake up.

Por que?

We need to stop for a smoke.

Okay. What do we do?

Just help me talk shit.

Okay.

Hey, Mr. Bus Driver, I kind of yell out.

Nothing.

Hey, Mr. Bus Driver, I say again. Hey.

Excuse me, sir. Mr. Bus Driver.

Nothing.

Excuse me, sir. Mr. Bus Driver, I say loud. And I'm loud. Not big, but loud. Started calling cadence the first day of boot camp. Our chief was like, Damn, boy, you got a big mouth. Fuckin' a.

Jesus jumps in. Hey, Mr. Bus Driver, he yells.

Mr. Fuckin' Bus Driver finally acknowledges our back-of-the-bus presence. He looks like the bus driver in Smoke Signals. Kick-ass moustache and all.

What's the problem? he says, with the "o" like an "aah," wit' dat accent like one of the Chicago Dennises, Franz or Farina. Either way, a bit of home. Weird.

We ask, Would it be cool if we stopped for a smoke break? Other heads on the bus whip around to look at me. I give some what's-up head-up nods to people I've been seeing on this ride. Which has been long. Which started in LA. Or Needles. Or Phoenix. Shit. I don't remember. But yeah, it's been going for a while.

The other folks on this bus, they say, Yeah. That's a gooood idea, Mr. Bus Driver.

He says, Well pipe down there, little man, we're almost to the stop.

Been hearing your *almost* shit for a while now, I say. I say, We should stop now, I think.

No, he says.

Yup, the other passengers say.

But, he says, we're almost there.

We're tired of your *almost* shit, too, they say. We're fixin' to stop right here, they say. Or we gonna light up right here on the bus.

Like y'all been doing in the bathroom? he says.

See. You ought to stop more, they say. You're turning us into crooks. Now pull over. Be a good guy, they say. Or we'll light *you* up too.

Goddamnit, he says. And pulls over.

We step off the bus out into the hot, dry air. People be lighting up like this was gonna be their last smoke ever, like maybe he wasn't really a bus driver but more their executioner, more that we were a pile of Gary Gilmores stuffed together in this rickety piece of shit and he's just hauling us out to the desert to put us down, mad dogs and refugees from all America never cared to give us. I think of Ralph Steadman sitting in a baked metal folding chair, sketching us as we debus and filling in the color over drinks and ether later on, and light up a Kool, hand out a couple more.

This bird goes by, walks/runs by so close I think it might have been on board with us. I look at its mouth to see if maybe it needed a smoke too and, sure enough, it looks like something's going on there in the shadow of the bus, she has something hanging out of her mouth; maybe a cig and not a French fry or something because the McDonalds is like seventeen miles away. Then she runs into the sun and I get a closer look and I see it's a green-and-white snake, and not a Newport 100. Hahaha. What the fuck kind of a bird eats snakes, for Chrissake?

Jesus, I say. Man. What the fuck is that?

He says, That's a roadrunner, bro.

Dang. That's a not good-looking bird, man.

No, he says. But it gets its bird job done.

How come it's not purple?

Como?

Well, aren't they supposed to be purple? And blue?

Seriously, bro? That's a cartoon. What's wrong with you?

Maybe that, I think. But I don't say anything.

We kick it for a bit, smoke two smokes each. Fuck that bus driver *and* his schedule. He eats free when we get to the McDonalds or the Burger King, so that's his payoff for getting him and us there, and whether he's alive or not probably matters even less to them than us, so we'll get there when we get there. I'm pretty sure one of us could drive this pile of crap. Shit, Goof drove a CTA bus home one night, so why not? He was waiting at the Broadway turnaround by Devon, like you always do, 'cause those fat fucks would go to this little convenience store that I think had a donut shack in the back, and they would be in there *forever*, and you'd be waiting to get the fuck out of Dodge, especially when you're slinking low in the back seat when four or five sȝupɥ would be walking by, and even though the police station is right down the street they just don't give a fuck, and how ignoble to die in the back of a greasy-windowed, piss-plowed, broke-ass-air-conditioned, sad-ass CTA bus?

One night Goof is sitting on the bus. Old boy driver is off eating donuts and, yeah, turns out it was actually a donut place—not the good Hostess ones, though, it was the one that was white with red and blue flowers, like on an Ojibway vest, like that cool beadwork they have, Homestead, or Homestyle, and Goof could see like six Corona putos coming down the street. He wasn't packing because he was getting all kinds of grief on the home front about banging because his ma was kind of tradish, always tryna get Goof to go to sweat or somethin' with her, so he gave his piece to Rondell to hold. Now he got nothing but a ass-load of sȝupɥ bout to see him through that window.

Fuck it, he thinks. Goof walks up to the front of the bus, looks out the big window, sees them sȝupɥ coming. They're not up to the police station yet, but they're about to be. Shit, he says. Hops in that big air-ride seat and looks around. Goof got a little of that OCD in him so he notices shit. And he likes to talk. Never fucking can shut up, seems like. So he had sat in the front of the bus a lot. Sat and talked to drivers on his way home late lots of nights. Watched everything they was doing. Knew there was an Allison automatic transmission. Saw the sign up top said 36 Broadway to Wells/Harrison, so all set there. Dude had even left his hat hanging off the little fan that was installed up by the mirror (guess he was a li'l sweaty and whatnot). Fuck it. *Tcshhhhhhhhhhh* goes the air when he releases the parking brake. He pops on the hat and gives the wheel a big swing to the right and to the left and he's out on Clark Street.

Goof is driving down the street and he's been on this bus a hundred times, so he goes ahead and makes the first pick up. Someone's waiting on Devon by the Golden Nugget, pronounced the Golden Noo-zhay by us hi-tone folks. Probably hoping the bus hurries so he doesn't crap his pants before he can make it home.

Goof pulls over and slow opens the door.

How you doing tonight, he says.

Fine, goes the customer / possible botulism victim.

Welcome aboard, Goof says, big grin and all.

The victim rolls his eyes around and holds his stomach a little.

Goof taps the fare box and says, it's broken, not working right tonight. You can just hand me the money. I'll give you an all-day transfer to make up for it, if you want.

I'm good, says the customer.

Yeah you are, says Goof with a weird leery look, totally out of place.

The guy grimaces and squeezes his guts while he makes his way to the back of the bus.

Goof smiles and eases on down the road.

He picks up fares and takes money. Hands out a couple of his "all-day transfers." Smokes cigarettes with his arm out the window. Passengers make faces at him, but whatever. He gets them where they're going. Makes his way down Broadway. After a while he finds himself in the neighborhood. He drops off a couple of hillbillies at Lawrence and heads through the intersection.

Almost home, he sings.

Pulls over at Leland. Flicks on the flashers. Alright, folks, he says. This bus is Out of Service. You all are gonna have to catch the next bus.

Should we get off the bus?

Nah. Not if you don't want to.

Where are you going? this lady asks.

Yeah, man, this guy says. Where are you going?

Home, man.

What?

Home, Goof says.

Shiiiit, the guy says.

Later, bro, Goof goes.

And he walks off down Leland toward his crib on Kenmore. Laughing like he did.

The cops came a couple hours later. They know him, knew it was him. Who else had that caved-in nose, Indian-long hair, fucked-up teeth with that accent, and that .45 tattooed on their arm? Didn't take them but about two minutes to figure out it was Goof and only a minute or two more to pick him up. Come on in, he said. I need to go back and get the other arm done anyway. Check out this tat, maing, he said. The cops didn't say nothing at all, just punched him in the stomach a couple times. Shut the fuck up, they said then, and dragged him out to the car. Goof laughed. But you know that shit hurt. It always will.

Jesus drags his ass back onto the bus. Tired, right? I tole you. Jesus is a tired motherfucker 'cause Jesus got two wives. One here some- where in America, and the other one in Mexico. Dude got like three jobs, too, but he says it's the wives that make his ass so tired. I believe that shit, too. I watch his face. He looks alone, and lonely too, and when his eyes go across the desert floor, deep and grey- blue, it looks like he's got no love, no nothing at all, the way his stare is so empty. You know. Just these wives and these jobs. Dude is ancient, oldt. Like twenty-eight. But he looks a hundred at least. I am not about that shit. I'll just ride and ride. I'd rather do my living out here, standing in the sun, watching this bird eat a snake, and get my face lined and my soul sanded down by wind and dust instead of by jobs and by judgment.

How do I know this shit about Jesus? 'Cause he told me when we met earlier. Probably didn't want to, or mean to, but people tell me shit all the time. The most personal shit you can imagine. I always wonder why that is. Is it because people trust me, or want me to like them? Or is it because people don't respect me, don't see me, just dump shit on me like I don't matter? I'll have to think about that one.

Jesus, though, he told me all this shit because old boy was drunk as a lord. I can make that assessment with a fair degree of accuracy 'cause so was I.

We're sitting in the back of the bus. Not all the way back where you have to see and smell the shitter every time someone goes in or out, but about three rows up, on the right-hand side of the bus. It's about 11:00 at night. I think we're near Deming, or that was the last stop, or the next one. It's kind of hot. Not too bad, but the air on this thing sucks. The batteries are running down on my Walkman, and I've been rewinding tapes with a pencil for the last couple of hours. I say fuckit and reach down in my bag (it's a bag forreal—I've got a hefty bag full of my clothes and some books, some tapes, and a sketch book and a notebook) and grab a beer. I've got about ten beers in there. They're pretty warm, but whatever. I'm on a bus.

I crack one open, tryna be all quiet I think, but not quiet enough, because this dude creaks his head around.

Hola, amigo. What you got there? Cervezas? Beers? You got any more?

Yeah, I say. A few.

Hunh. Maybe I could get one?

Only got a few, homes, I say.

He says, That's cool. We can trade a li'l.

I say, Trade what?

He says, Tequila.

Shit, man. I think to myself, I don't know if I want to drink some fuckin' tequila. Man, last time I drank tequila was back in Phoenix. The bartender at this place I used to go would save up the worms from the mezcal bottles for me. One night I went in there and he's like, Hey, man! Got like five worms here for you. Cool, I say. Throw 'em in a shot for me, would ya?

For sure, he says.

I down this shot with these fuckin' worms along with four more or so and I eat like six vivarins and then I play foosball. This gigantic drunk dude is all,

Hey, fucker. I will beat your ass in foos.

I'm like, I don't think so, ya jolly bastard.

What, he says? Let's play for drinks.

I say,

Okay, but I hope your ass is that fat 'cause your wallet is full. You're fixin' to lose some dough, bro.

I proceed to beat the shit out of this guy, but he's getting really pissed off. I take like four games in a row and he's doing the desperation doubling up. Now he owes me a lot. I'm thinking this dude don't lose that often, when he decides to tell me that HE IS THE FUCKING PIMA INDIAN CHAMPION OF FOOSBALL AND PROBABLY THE WORLD AND THAT HE IS GOING TO WHUP MY ASS, and ever since I was a little kid like in fourth grade I can't take people yelling in my face, and all of a sudden the bartender, Señor Gusano there, appears on my right with a pool cue. What the fuck, I think, that seems pretty convenient, and then I wake up like twenty minutes later on the floor in the back of the bar.

I feel around for a minute. Both of my hands work, but the knuckles are all creaky. That's good, I think. That they work, yeah, and that I must've landed some punches because, well, that's all coming back in a flood. My face is a little swole under my eye, but the nose seems to be okay for once. I'm tasting some saltiness, but my tongue tells me all of the teeth I went under with are still there, and the ones that were missing to begin with aren't filled with anything they shouldn't be. The top of my head feels okay, but when I check out the back, my hand comes away sticky. Okay. I feel around. Shit. There's some grit, and maybe an old cigarette butt or something, or a peanut, or a candy corn—what the fuck?—but no fresh blood. Good, because, hey, no money for stitches, and I don't have anyone around here who could do it for me anyway, even if I showed them how. How do I know how to do stitches? Shit, man. Read a book. And practice.

I listen for a bit, but there's no one around me, no one talking shit. Classic rock is on because of the shitty DJ at the radio station they play in here, but everyone who works there drinks here, so we deal with it, but there are one or two cats who'll play some newer shit if you promise to buy them a shot later, so yeah. It kind of hurts when I breathe, so I probably at least cracked a couple ribs. Finally I open one, then the other eye. No crazies around, people are just chillin' at the bar, and the foosball table is empty. I don't see those dudes anywhere, so either they're in the bathroom holding hands together and peeing and I'm about to get jumped any minute, or they're gone for the night. I take my chances and head for the bar.

Hahaha! Craig laughs. What the hell, bro! That was nuts!

Gimme a beer, I say.

Hold on, man. Don't you want a shot? he laughs again.

Fuck you, dude, I say. Gimme a beer, man.

Okay, okay, he says. Here you go.

Dude, I say. Stop giving me those fuckin' worms. And did you hand me a cue stick?

Yeah. About that. Sorry, man. Threw a little dust in there with those worms. My bad, he says.

I oughta kick your ass too, ya big sumbitch, I laugh.

Really though, I hate this Texas fucker with his Ogilvie Home Perm and his copstache. He's a real prick, but he likes to buy me drinks. Whatever.

So what happened, anyway, I ask.

Hahaha, he says. That big dude tried to grab you up and you smashed him in the face with the cue stick. His nose made this really cool and awful sound, and then he started yelling, and his buddy cracked you in the back of the head with a bottle.

Is that how I got this gash back here? I say.

No, he laughs. That shit bounced off your head and hit that scrawny little fucker in the face. He went down over there. What the hell is your melon made out of, man? Concrete? Holy shit that was funny.

So how did I get my head laid open? I ask.

He says, Well, when you hit big boy, he was coming for your neck with everything he had plus both hands, and you fucked him up so good with the stick he got knocked out then kind of fell and bounced on top of you and rolled off to the side. Your head hit the ground good when you two went down, and it made this *whack!* sound.

So then what happened? I say.

The best part.

What was that?

He says, Man, you were pissed. You were holding your ribs on the one side but you were yelling louder than anyone I've ever heard. I thought for sure you were gonna wake those two mother-fuckers up, but you never did.

Is that it? I say.

No, man. Like I said, he says, it was the best part of the night. 'Cause while you were standing there yelling at the top of your lungs you just cocked your leg up on the end of the bench in the booth, straight whipped it out, and started pissing on the big guy. Holy fuck, I thought for sure they're gonna wake up now, but they never did, even when you were laughing and shaking it out on his partner.

Jesuschrist.

What the hell is wrong with me, I thought.

So, is that it? I say.

Hahaha. Is that it, he says, says Craig. Yeah, I guess so, you crazy sonofabitch. Hey. Let's drink. The rest of the night is on me, he says. Best shit I've seen in a long time.

So, yeah. I was thinking tequila was probably not the best thing to drink while confined to the back of a bus rolling between all of hell's circles, but hey, maybe it would help the warm beer taste better, right?

Okay, homes, I say. Let's trade.

I say,

Let's *drink*.

PUSH IT

Introduction

I used to think about Los Angeles a lot. I lived in Chicago then, but I never thought about that. I thought about LA. Denver. Hollywood. Phoenix. Needles. The Salton Sea. Yreka. The Pacific Coast Highway. The Southwest Chief. Sun. Sky. Vistas. Horizons. Mountains. Purple. Grey. Blue. White. Yellow. Tangerine. Warm air. At night.

Warm air at night.

When I would think about warm air at night, I would think about the Griffith Park Observatory. In black, grey, purple-hued blue, and white. Like in *Rebel Without a Cause*. I never saw the whole movie until I was way older, but whenever I did see it on Channel 7 (not like, say, *Cooley High*, which I saw, I don't know, at least eight times beginning to end) it was always this one scene that would fade in, and I'd have to stop and watch because that super-black black night, and the warm white-grey light, and those palm trees swaying and rustling, hustling up this dream of something California had to offer to a stuck-ass, skinny-ass, running-out-of-luck-ass kid in the middle of the city, a husky Midwestern city, humid and cold and icy and grey, salty street spraying mud in your eye every day, well, yeah. How could you not watch?

You could feel the warm air through the TV.

Smell the night-blooming flowers.

Hear the rolling ocean.

See the widening future right on the faces of those actors, Sal and James and Natalie, those shortish but still fine-looking boys and that beautiful, beautiful girl; a future they never knew how good they would miss, and the world would make them die young just to make sure,

and after that scene played out, you turned away as the cops showed up, and thought about the parents on their way, and were like

these kids could be make-believe parents too someday, less than zero parents, sure, but they'll have kids of their own, and they'll live in nice houses, ones with year-round azaleas and pools and tiled roofs, and they'll have that warm air at night and, shit, well I want that too, how the fuck is it these people get that, claim that, own that, like it was left at their doorstep and they just had to take it, no questions asked? Where and what, after all, is justice but someone taking some goddamn initiative any goddamn way?

Part I

In Chicago, a few years later:

Sure, I'll hitch a ride with you, I say.

Heading to New Orleans? Maybe LA?

I can do that.

What a fucking ride this is. The guy I'm hitching from is a total asshole. I can't believe I'm stuck with this prick for how many miles? He has one of those fucked-up names, where you don't know where the first one ends and the last one begins, so you never really know what to call him. I watch him watch himself in the rearview mirror. I flip open the rusty passenger side triangle window and light a smoke.

Shiiiiiit.

Mississippi. Cicadas and rednecks drone on. Misty air everywhere. Like fog in the sun. Green beyond green. Trees wider than trailers. Gas stations down here look like gas-station bathrooms do back home. I haven't eaten in a day or so but probably couldn't if I wanted to. Well, okay, I do want to, but I can't. I'm already broke. Fuck.

Okay. Not totally broke. I've got about twelve bucks.

We pull into some town south of Jackson off of I55. Bogue Chitto, maybe.

Handsome Boy says, I'm going to drive around for a bit. I'll drop you here so you can eat, but I'll be back in an hour.

Okay, I think. Whatever the fuck that's all about.

Sure, I say. See you then.

And I think, If he ditches me, I'll track him down. Guaranteed.

I walk around. Well, I walk down these broiled, sticky roads and try not to get hit.

There's no sidewalks.

I think, Man. I might die here.

For real.

I'm walking down this county highway. It's a hot-top black snake, blind corners, walls of green on either side. Bugs whirr. Haze hangs in soggy white clumps from dark wet branches. I can't imagine there's been a breeze through here since marauding Yankees dragged cannons over this horseshit-stained hump in the road sometime last century. Twenty-year-old cars chug by every now and again; fat, white, fleshy arms hang out of their windows and the chunky, red hands on their ends slap out time on rusty pock-marked green, orange, and primer-colored doors to country songs that America has long forgotten. Suspicious eyes check out my long hair and pretty brown self and slow on the downshift without ever hitting the brakes. I shudder like it's five degrees out and mosey on, deeply interested in either the ditches on the side of the highway or the shoes on my feet, depending on the turns in the road and the proximity of my observers. Now I keep to the grass.

The humidity. For fuck's sake. It's so hazy and damp and now so smelling like cigarette smoke and sour beer I feel like I'm walking through some kind of giant, open-air tavern from back in the '50s. And I think I see a "For Whites Only" water fountain somewhere up ahead, so yeah. Perfect. The sun hangs overhead, somehow invisible but making its presence felt by cranking the heat up to danger-this-pressure-cooker-is-about-to-explode levels. How the fuck do people live here? It's *April* for Chrissake. The ground is soaked and barely holding up all this wet. My feet sink a little with each step, just like my heart, and I think maybe I'll just fall through in a minute here because why not, anything is probably better than what's probably going on up ahead.

And that's no lie. I come around yet another turn in the road and look up to see a blindingly white ass crack staring at me through an open door. Hilarious. Sitting on top of a stool the guy probably nailed his legs to, it looks like two frogs belly-to-belly fucking where I couldn't see their faces up under the red, white, and blue plaid shirt or their feet shoved down into the wranglers. More cracks of ass march down the bar, shitkicker boots hang onto rickety stools for dear life, liberty, the pursuit of happiness, and a TV fishing show with the sound turned down because what the fuck would you talk about out there anyway? And what is this place? I look left to right, and I'll be damned. Apparently, one of these wily peckerwoods has turned his or her double-wide into a bar. Glasses clink and Charley Pride pleads for release from this shithole through screened and barred windows that collect horse-flies and moths along with the rent souls of patrons who can never quite leave and probably wouldn't bother given even half the chance. Where the fuck would you go, anyway?

Mr. Anchoring Ass Crack himself is parked under an enormous Confederate battle flag, its folds casting dark shadows on the racks of Yankee pork rinds that are slowly finishing off the war his ancestors started. Hanging bags of nuts watch a couple of grimy-ass hotdogs roll around in their own misery, or, sorry, no, haha, those are just the assembled patrons I'm seeing in the bar-length mirror that runs across the back of the Buggered Plough-man, or the Fatted Calf, or the Dead-Eyed Yokel, or whatever the fuck the name of this place is. It's pretty rowdy for a Thursday. Must be the first of the month. Or the day they bring the prettiest pigs to town. Either way, all this hoopin' and a-hollerin' can only mean there's gonna be plenty of cousin-fucking later on tonight, and I pick up the pace. Desperation, racism, and crack(er) sweat eep out across the doorstep and from the foundation. I huff up all three as I hustle on by, shaking my head, trying to clear it of these wretched and ancient Confederate spirits.

As I walk I have to ask myself, Should I have gone in, had a chat, made a buddy, tried to offer some semblance of redemption to that chubby and somehow-not-so-banal disciple of sibilant and persistent racism? And if I did, to whose benefit would it have been? Mine, so that I can feel good about humanity, or myself, or myself as a human? His? I can't really see redemption or him understanding its possibility happening for him, short of his life being threatened in some way. Redemption certainly eludes the willfully ignorant, and it has a hell of a time reaching the structur-ally benighted. Since I took a pass on the whole potential drama and quick-stepped down the road, I'll have only myself to blame should some neo-Wallace type win a presidential election by a single vote someday. I'll take that chance. I'm not as good a person as I like to tell myself I am, but then again, I survive.

I come around one more of these endless goddamn bends in the road, and lo and behold, it's a store. It's made out of . . . metal, I guess. Lots of rust on rust on silver and silver paint. A wizened box of bolts and duct tape lurches and wheezes around in a shallow-panned frame attached to the side of the whole pile of shit; I suppose that at least in theory it's there to keep the place cool, but it would appear to do naught else but dribby drab warm water and keep the state electric company in the black while providing much needed respite for cottonmouths. I approach it all with extreme caution.

I ring the requisite brass bell on my way through the front door. I know the big ding is coming, but it startles me anyway. The quiet in here is right out loud. The buzzing that I think is coming from some despicable fluorescent light is actually the humidity trying to drown me on the fly. And underneath it, there's this other noise. As I pay attention to it, hone in on it with my bionic bartender ear, I realize I've erred most fatally, and I'm now stuck with the incessant concatenations of a million fucking crickets.

The tiredest black woman I've ever met in my life looks me up and down, even slower than this humidity that is killing me one relentless second after another. I meet her eye. We're just cute, with our matching blue bandannas.

MmmmHmmmm, she says.

UnnnnnHunnnnnh, I say.

Well, she says.

Yes, ma'am, I say.

Ma'am, I continue, are those crickets I'm hearing?

They are.

All day? Every day?

Yessir. Come have a look, she says.

We walk over to a big old fish tank.

Hunh, I say.

She looks at me.

Well, I say, what do you feed a cricket?

A little bit of sugar, she says,

and some

whiiiiiiite

potato.

I laugh at that. Shiiiiiiit, I say. And you have to listen to them day and night?

Day and night, she says.

What are they for? I ask.

Bait, baby. They're just bait.

She licks her lips and rings up my Suzy-Qs.

I eat with great joy and abandon. Hostess is the shit, that's no lie, and if I'd had to eat Little Debbie's I would've passed. But Handsome Boy better find me quick, I think. I'm ready to get the fuck out of here.

He shows up after a while. La-dee-da and all. Shit, I think. This motherfucker. I have visions of sacrificing that face of his on the wheel of this ancient road god, this Dodge Titan we're driving around in, and then I remember that we're in the South, AND I don't have a license. Sonofabitch. I'd get about ten miles max, and then I'd be dreaming about Paul Newman, George Kennedy, hard-boiled eggs, and the hotbox. Man. I got other shit to do.

I keep my mouth shut, say what's up, and go sit in the back, where it's apparently my job to make this camper as hot as possible, and I am kicking ass on the TPS reports. Damn it. I really hate this Handsome Boy motherfucker. But you know what? It gets better. We get pulled over in Las Cruces, New Mexico.

Let me tell you what happens.

First, we have to start in New Orleans. And this shit is fucked up. Dude fucks up his transmission on the way down. What did he do? I still have no idea. Left the parking brake on or something. But we end up in this junkyard while dudes be looking for a replacement piece. They say it might be a week.

Handsome Boy, he says, Well, fuck you, more or less. I got money, and I'm going to town. Taking this chick with me.

I say, Yeah, whatever, have a good time, because what else am I going to say? 'Bout an hour later this dude comes out to the camper.

Hey, man.

Hey, man. What's up?

Boss says you cain't stay here. Closing up. Gone let the dogs out.

It's cool, I say. I was gonna stay in the camper.

Cain't do that, man, he says.

Well shit. What am I gonna do? I say.

Got to go, brother.

Got no money, I say. Nothing.

Be back, he says.

He comes back about twenty minutes later. He says,

Got the hat gone around. Maybe two, t'ree dollar here. Gone give it to you.

For what? I say.

De bus, he says.

Man, what bus?

He says, To de city, man.

Okay, I say.

Well, he says, got a catch wit' it.

What? I say.

He says, Ever meet a Cajun, well, got to do right by them. We ain't got much money, but dis here yours, he says.

It's a deal, brother, I say.

'ere you go.

I take the money, hop on the bus. Go downtown New Orleans, Mardi Gras, Fattest of Tuesdays. I got one dollar left after the bus.

Me, I go to Jean Lafitte's bar. Buy one beer. Watch this old lady play piano.

This handsome white man says, Hey, boy. What doin'?

I say, Nothin' much. Got no funds.

He says, Got skills?

I say, Man. I paint faces. That's about it.

Take this twenty dollar, he says. Pay me back.

Okay, I say.

Off to the Piggly Wiggly across Canal I go. Buy some face paint. Go downtown.

I do dragons mostly, some snakes, and a wolf. Five bucks a crack. Five more for two or more colors. I make about a hundred dollars.

Back to Lafitte's I go.

Pay the man. Double that money, give him forty dollars.

He says, I knew you be good for dis. Good job, bwai.

I'm glad to pay.

I sleep in an unlocked car by the Andrew Jackson Hotel. I wake up with a sunburn on one side of my face and frostbite on the other. I stumble down Royal. Up Decatur. Walk by Café du Monde. This old black man sees me and says, Damn, bwai. Ya look rough. Take this dollar. By som'tin to eat, yeah?

Okay, I say. Thanks.

I buy a beignet. Man. Ever have a beignet from the Café du Monde? Bucket list that shit.

We hang out in New Orleans for a while, separately, though, yeah. One day, back I go to the junkyard. Find Handsome Boy. All smart this fucker is. We take off in the big camper. Not so smart, though, that he don't take off the parking brake. By Del Rio, Texas, his transmission is fucked.

I walk around town. I wear boots, because #fuckrattlesnakes. This older white lady I meet by the garage that's going to do the work on Handsome Boy's camper takes a shine to me. Buys me the best chicken fried steak I've ever had. Doesn't try to fuck me, so that's nice. Gives me some smokes and five bucks. Alright.

Handsome Boy gets his transmission fixed. Must be nice to have a bank account. Anyway, off we go, back on the road, parking brake disengaged. The girl has left. Must be getting tan and needs to get her white ass home. I think her name was Kim, but then that might be every white chick I've ever met.

We pull into Las Cruces. Border Patrol yanks us over. Handsome Boy is freaking out, but I don't know why. I'm like, Welcome to America, fucker. Whateeeeeever.

Then I figure out the issue. See, when we were in New Orleans, Handsome Boy was so handsome (and greedy) he got himself a job working at a Hurricane stand. I go to the stand one night, and this white guy is buying a drink. Ugly fucking white guy—rugby shirt, homemade passed-out-at-a-party haircut, blond stubble, big mouth like a fish. He's buying a drink, but he drops a paper package when he pulls his money out. Handsome Boy (Greedy Boy), he sees it right away, points it out. I step on it, and when Ugly Boy leaves, I pick it up. It's about a gram and a half of coke. Ugly Boy must have done a couple of decent-sized lines out of a sixteenth and then shoved it in his pocket. Handsome Boy knows I have it, and that's that.

Because I'm locked up in the mobile home while we've been on our way across Texas, and Handsome Boy and Kimmy have been staying in hotels, I did some of the coke. Handsome Boy (Greedy Boy) is going to be pissed, and I still have to get to California. I've been thinking, Shit—how am I going to explain this?

Careful what you wish for, motherfucker, because, well, yeah.

We get pulled over by La Migra.

At Las Cruces, Handsome Boy sweats off two or three pounds. That'll help him in Hollywood, I guess. I whistle to myself, because, well, yeah, wtf. The border cops do a lot of yelling, but I know they're just looking for illegals crabbed onto the bottom of this camper, or whatever. Handsome Boy, though, I think he crapped his pants. The cops say, You got like five minutes or whatever, and then we're coming in. I go to the back of the camper and grab the coke, put it in the change pocket of my jeans. La Migra says, If you got anything in there, you better tell us now! Handsome Boy gulps and says, Whatbouthecoke?

I say, Just shut up, and don't say nothing.

He says, They'll take my camper if they find the coke.

Not if it's on me, asshole, I say.

You'd take the fall? he says.

Take the fall? This ain't a fuckin' movie, I say. Just shut up already.

Come on out, they say.

We head out and over to the office. Dogs follow us.

Holy shit, man, he says. Fuckin' dogs.

I say, I got dog medicine. Just be *quiet* already.

We sit in the office for about twenty minutes, La Migra trying to sweat us.

No illegals though, so they don't really give a fuck. But they bring in the dogs anyway.

This big shepherd looks at me like he wants to make out. The Rottweiler sits next to my left leg and we exchange dog talk. La Migra says to get the fuck out of here, so we do.

We hop in the camper. Handsome Boy is having a stroke or whatever.

Holy shit, man, he says. Where is that coke?

In my pocket, dickhead, I say.

What are we gonna do? he says.

We? I say. We, nothing. I, on the other hand, am doing this—and I take the seal, open it, and do all the coke at once. Man, I was so high. Fuck you, Handsome Boy. I smoked, like, my last three cigarettes and then I don't know what. Good times, I guess. But not for him.

Eventually we got to LA, and Handsome Boy and I parted ways. He hung around for a while, insulted my friends, went on auditions, and then gave up and left after a couple of weeks. About two days after he was gone, the callbacks started coming in. Hilarious. Dude would've had all kinds of work. But because he was an asshole and didn't leave a forwarding number, #fuckthatguy. Oh well.

I moved to LA to . . . move to LA, and figure out the music business. My best buddy played guitar, taught me some stuff on bass, and we went to shows, telemarketed, hung out with other musician types, and starved a lot. That's part of the music biz. But if you're good, and you're related to somebody, or know somebody who isn't afraid to put themselves in the right place at the right time, well, you might just make it. That's the other part.

There's a whole lot of other story that goes in here, and though I never did get to the Griffith Park Observatory, it's not about that anyway, and right now, looking at this word count, we need to move things along.

Part II

More music biz stuff. Now I'm a band manager. Producer. Show promoter. Booking agent. Life is . . . musical. This is like 1991, Chicago. Wicker Park. SXSW is starting to get going, so up north here someone decides to put on something called MWMC, the Mid-West Music Conference.

I kinda work for this entertainment/production company, but really I just do what I want, big surprise. Plus try to write, and bartend, and side projects, and tour with my boys. But this conference, well, the guy who owned the company thought we should definitely go. He had all the promo material spread out on our rickety desks in our "offices," which was really the living room of his dumpy apartment on Thomas Street between Ashland and Milwaukee. There were going to be a bunch of shows, all different kinds of music at clubs and venues all over the city. I look at some of the joints listed on the program, places I've never been, like China Club downtown and shit. I say, Sure, whatever, how much is it? Ziggy (because pale as Stardust) says in his terrible just-above-a-munchkin-range voice that it won't cost us a thing, and that all the bands we book/manage are pitching in to pay our way. Okay, cool, I think.

I say,

You're sure they know? 'Cause you're kind of a bullshitter.

He assures me they're on board, so I take his word for it.

Aside from being a bullshitter, you need to know that this guy was a huge cokehead. I mean a clammy, sweaty, waxy, way-too-high-every-time-he-did-it cokehead, and those people are really no fun. And they don't like to share.

He talked about how going to this conference would put the company on the map, set us up in Chicago, blahblahblah, and how he couldn't wait to go, but it seemed to me that what he really wanted was what he always wanted, which was a bunch of coke, all to himself. We prepped hard for this thing (meaning we got some T-shirts made up), and sure enough the day before the whole thing is going to start he hits me up, asks can I get us some decent coke, says he doesn't want to buy the usual stepped-all-over bullshit from Birdman in the bar where we sort of work.

I say, Well no, not really, unless you're going for quantity.

Oh yeah, totally, he says.

How much? I ask.

Like a quarter?

No.

A half ounce?

I guess. But you still have to work, you know. You can't just be high, gumming away at people and shit. This is business, man.

Yeah. I know. How much? he asks.

I'm making a little on this too, so I say, Eight hundred.

Seriously? he says.

Yeah, I say.

Is it any good? he asks.

I say, Don't insult me again, fucker. And don't act like that in my old neighborhood. Or you'll never make that conference. Show some respect.

I have to go with?

Yeah, you do. If some shit goes down, that package is in your hand, not mine.

Fuck.

See you tomorrow. I'm taking the rest of the day off.

Well shit. Next day I'm thinking about how to get way up to the far North Side. We live in the city, so no one has a car. Okay, my buddy's girlfriend Julie has a little pickup truck that her dad picked out for her, but he picked one with a manual transmission figuring none of her drunk-ass dirtbag pals or boyfriends from the city could drive it and fuck it up. Psych. This dirtbag right here got his license in Oklahoma, so yeah, I can drive a stick. But we had four or five people, so that wouldn't work. Then Ziggy says,

Oh yeah, hey, we're getting a limo for the night.

Hahahaha.

Okay, big man, I say. But we gotta get going if you want to pick up that shit.

Alright, he says. I'll have the car come get us right now.

Great, I say, and smoke cigarettes, and stare at Ziggy, and wonder how someone could be so blindingly white, like snowy paraffin, like Elric of Melniboné, but with dyed burgundy-tangelo hair, a castoff muppet who should taste like those orange-raspberry popsicles they used to have at the Good Humor truck, but you know he's just sour and smells like moldy walnuts and spoiled mayonnaise. The minutes tick by and he sweats silently. Not like sweat rolls off him, but just sort of sssseeeeps out of him, appears in tiny beads that are the color of the almost-done fluid from a nasty zit; not quite clear but you're not sure why not, what the composition of that fluid is. Like that.

I shiver and keep an eye out the window of our street-level office, chew the inside corner of my lip, and will the limo into existence.

The man we'd soon know as Vassily shows up with our ride just in the nick of time; Ziggy has worked his fingernails into bloody little half-moons. Shit that must hurt, I think. A couple more minutes and he would've been chewing his girlfriend's cuticles. I look over at his waxy ass and say,

Get a grip, man. The car's here.

We head up to my old neighborhood, driven by super-friendly Vassily (I tell him my name and he says, T'e, T'eyo, fuck. Like Fyodor? You are not writer are you? Please say no or I will leave you in bad neighborhood), a kind of linguist/Uki/Russkie gangster with a crazy mustache that looks like a shop-floor broom, who, on the way up north, regales us with tales of being a former professor of linguistics in the Soviet Union along with escapades of his shady "modeling agency." (And assures us, Just driving heap of shit to make extra money go home, and buy, uh, and *recruit*, more model. As a note, all of his spoken "h's" come with little guttural "x's" in front—this accent of his—he's like a potty-mouthed Yakov Smirn-off . . .)

I have him go up Milwaukee Avenue to Western. I want to drive by Rosehill Cemetery. We used to go fishing in the ponds and get chased by the spooky custodians. Those guys were creepy, but they didn't have shit on some of the people buried up in there. Beside a bunch of mayors and sausage-baron dudes (Oscar Mayer and Swift, guys like that, guys who gentrified Wicker Park the *first* time around), Charles Hull is there. He's the guy who gave Hull House to Jane Addams, and they say that's the house where the baby who would become the story behind *Rosemary's Baby* was born (shuddershudder if you were a kid in the '70s and saw *that* movie "on accident").

But my thoughts quickly turn to modern-day horror as I start to tune into whatever Vassily is going on about up front.

Dude. I don't want to know those things about you, I say. I don't want to hear any more about how you love Babyface or want to manage your own boy band. Roll up that goddamn divider before I page your boss, I say, and turn off that motherfucking Jodeci before I light this backseat on fire, Stalin.

What saying, fucker? he says to me. Thinking you can just talk the shit with your dirty Polack accent and fat Indian face?

What, motherfucker? I can't believe this guy is talking all this smack. Hilarious. I laugh and crack a beer from the bag I brought. It was an Old Style or a Modelo, and it was friggin' delicious.

No drinking in here, greasy face.

Fuck you, DP, I say, and start to *whirrrrrr* up the divider.

I catch his eye and six gold teeth in his laugh in the rearview mirror as the glass closes.

I quick flip him the bird before it gets to the top, and laugh myself.

We fly through the wide, dirty streets of the North Side, Ziggy ravaging his cuticles and dampening the seats.

Pull over right up here, Vassily.

What? You're smoking the dope, man. Is no way. Too tight.

Shiiiiit. Don't lie. You could fit this, six of your "models," and a potato harvester or whatever you used to drive, plus the donkey you were married to right there with room to spare.

Are such big asshole, man. How long going to be gone?

I look out the window, look up and down the block. People are hanging out on the stoops, staring down at this big Linc. Pointing. Talking. Shit.

Ten minutes, tops. I'll leave Ziggy here with you. You can explore the long-term debilitating effects of cocaethylene on the speech function of transparent Americans.

Hahaha. Hurry up, fuckerface. Are too cute. Vassily will miss you.

Put those handcuffs away, Captain KGB. I'll be back in a minute.

I high-five him and head into the building.

I bounce back out in about ten. Vassily, driver cap and all, opens that big town-car door for me. Proper. The neighborhood watches.

I get comfy. Crack another beer. Vassily raises a wild eyebrow up front, but wisely keeps his opinions on greasy faces drinking in Lincolns to himself.

Vassily. Want a line?

Does Pope shit in wood?

Ziggy appears to be having particularly severe heart palpitations, or he's trying to keep from shitting his pants. I can't really tell, but soon enough, Heyyyy, he says, in that now severely constricted Unc Nunkie voice of his, what are you doing, man?

What? I say, and jam a rolled up twenty right into the bag and offer the other end to Vassily.

Heyyyy. Fuck you. Don't give that to him.

Vassily pops off. Shut up, head of popsicle, face of зима. This is tip for my fine driving.

Yeah. Calm down, man. There's enough to kill even you in here, I say. You need to learn how to share, fuck-o.

Yeah, fuck-o, Vassily says. Sharing is caring, my American friend.

Ziggy's face pulls in on itself like a blanched flytrap, makes those eyes that Gollum would make in a movie one day, the one when someone gets hold of *his* precious. It ain't pretty.

I offer a nervous laugh and say, Relax, Holmes. Here. Hit this shit. Vassily, take us to the Vic.

Theater by Belmont and Sheffield? he asks.

That's the one, Jeeves. Step on it, I say.

Vassily don't know who this fucking Jeeves is, but Vassily is paid for night, so stepping on it is not any kind problem. And this кокаин from Vassily new greasy-face friend is good. Very good. Will like to drive fast now. Right now.

Holy moly. His jaw is working like it's getting paid time and a half. I'm a little worried for my suddenly lightweight companions. Ziggy is staring out the window, finger tapping out guitar exercises written by St. Vitus or Paganini or some shit, and Vassily is rubbing his face so much he's starting to get a rash.

Vassily.

Da?

Stop that, man. Stop rubbing at your face. You're going to hurt yourself.

Is fine. Is no big deal. Vassily thinking.

You should have a drink or something, man.

This drinking in car upset Vassily. You know this, Vassily new friend Dostoyevsky. Do not trifle with rules. Do not try corrupt young vanguard revolution.

He winks/leers/flashes three or four of those gold teeth.

Jesus. Fucking communists. Ziggy. Give Vassily a Valium or something. Lookit that vein on the side of his head.

Heyyyy. No way. I've only got a few.

Don't be that way, man. Give him a half at least. Remember our talk about learning to share. He's fixing to explode. You don't want to die, do you?

Fuckin' Ayyyy. Fine.

Ziggy pulls out this grimy looking pill bottle, shakes out a little blue tab on the closed metal ashtray above the door handle, razor-blades its crease, cuts it perfectly in half, and hands it through the divider. I say, Hey, Vassily, here's a beer to wash it . . .

Vassily chews that half a 10 like it's a fucking Tic Tac. Jeezus-christ.

I don't know how they did shit in Russia, but . . .

Is Ukraine.

Okay. Ukraine. Whatever. I don't know how you all did shit over there, maybe you didn't have potable water or whatnot, but in America we take our pills with some kind of beverage. Hope I don't see that again.

Stop trying to get Vassily high, homeboy, take advantage this beautiful man. Then Vassily not have to take anti–heart attack pill.

I laugh.

Ziggy grimaces.

I tsk-tsk his motherfucking albino ass and say to the front of the car,

Hey, Vassily.

What now, Dostoyevsky? Why bothering poor Vassily?

I've been missing you. Hey. Do you know who we're going to see at the Vic?

He glances at me in his rearview.

Can only imagine, boss man. What decadent American who has sold principles and honor of own mother for five dollar is Dostoyevsky going to enjoy while poor Vassily park in alley and huff diesel fume from opulent mobile shrine to capitalism called tour bus?

Marky Mark and the honest-to-god-motherfucking Funky Bunch.

He says, Of course you are. Vassily not surprised at all. This sound like nightmare of Western depravity: shitty musician, manufacture beats and hype, girls, and all kinds excess. Right up you alley, boss.

I say, Jesus Christ. Lighten up, Francis.

Vassily don't know Francis. But fuck him too.

Line, Vassily?

Of course.

Ziggy moans a little, like he's trapped in a bad dream.

Fuck, man. I'm surrounded by the touchiest fucking people on earth.

We get to the Vic Theater, and I tell Vassily to park in the alley next to it and to see if he can fit out back under the El. I run my hands through my hair, blow out a pile of air. I open a beer and chug the whole thing. Now Vassily is tsk-tsking, the judgey bastard. I have to get the fuck out of here. This is killing my buzz.

I say, Well, get to huffing, Vassily. We're going inside. Enjoy your lot in life for embracing communism.

I fucking hate you so much, Dostoyevsky. Hoping you catch venereal disease.

Fuck you, too, Vassily. I hope the one I got from your mom kills off whatever I pick up in here.

You are asshole, that's for sure.

But the one employing you, *that's* for sure. Don't go nowhere, now.

He winks at me.

I wink back and head down the alley toward the front of the Vic. Ziggy toddles along beside me.

Jeezuschrist. What is my life?

Me and Ziggy have a horrible time. We're not really friends, so whatever, saw that coming. I watch the show. Sort of. The Funky Bunch. The Wahlberg. Yeah. I'm more interested in watching the bouncers/roadies grabbing up the girls selected by the band, bringing them backstage. Vassily was right. About everything. God, this is awful. I finally give zero fucks, do coke and shots of Jäger right there on the main floor, pound three or four Rolling Rocks, and say, Hey, man. Let's get the fuck out of here. Ziggy seems genuinely relieved and is starting to even out a bit. Good, I think. Because I am *not* resuscitating that fucker. I shudder a little. Ziggy looks at me and I *know* he knows *exactly* what I was just thinking about. He smiles, and I see his grey teeth. I shudder a little more and head for the door, Ziggy staring at the floor and loping along behind me.

C'mon, you undead fucker. Let's move it, I say.

Heyyyy. That's not cool.

Shit, man. I want to get the hell out of here. Don't you want to do a blast and head downtown?

Well, yeah, he says, his face unpuckering even more.

The way to this man's heart is probably right through that big vein in his thigh, but thank God we haven't gotten there yet.

Vassily! What the fuck are you doing?!

Shiiiiit.

I smack the driver's side window.

Vassily! Are you in there rubbing one out?

No.

Really? Then what the hell is going on?

Vassily drop cherry from cigarette in lap. Is trying to put out.

With a bunch of lotion? I ask.

Well, Vassily anticipating burn. Preventive medicines.

Goddamn, Vassily. Just . . . finish up, for fuck's sake. We'll be out here.

Me and Ziggy do lines on the trunk of the limo. We're parked in the alley behind the Vic. I don't know how Vassily got in here, but I hope he can get out. We lean on the car and drink beer. Vassily is taking forever—too much coke—so Ziggy and me make small talk about the mostly shitty but sometimes great bands we handle, and I flip off the Ravenswood line yuppies riding home to the neighborhoods they're just starting to ruin. I take a quick leak, shake it at some Gordon Gecko–looking fuck, and smack the roof of the car.

Let's fucking go, Vassily!

Ziggy looks at me like he just remembered I was here and says, Heyyyyyy. Are you going to give me my shit or what?

This? I say, holding the baggie. I thought we were splitting it, but that's cool. You take it.

No, no. We can split it, he says.

I already took out a gram or so back inside the bathroom in the Vic. I involuntarily pat the change pocket of my pants where it rests comfortably inside the folded-up twenty that'll probably be my cab fare from wherever I wake up tomorrow.

It's good, I say. You take it. I'll hang on to my cash. Just turn me on and I'll get the drinks. This, by the way, is an *excellent* deal for me—I rarely if ever have to buy a drink. As a bartender, I know . . . all the other bartenders.

Heyyyyy. Okay, fine, Ziggy says.

Alright, Vassily! That's it. You'll have to hold it 'til we get to our next spot.

And what den of capitalist excess will Dostoevsky be shedding last bit of dignity in? asks Vassily, zipping up his black polyester sansabelts.

China Club.

Is opium den?

I mock him in his own accent. Is opium den? What the fuck, Vassily? Is 1860?

Vassily does not know these things. Vassily not dirty imperialist. Also, education about West end with theft of land and resource from first great Marxist people, Red Indians. Notice, "Red." Red like beautiful flag Soviet Union. Indians Marxist.

Well, shit, man, I say. I wish. I say this about at least a couple of things.

Anything possible, in America, says Vassily.

Not this time, Khruschhev. It's just a cheesy club.

Fine, boss. Where is this typical deceptive name Yankee shithole?

Head downtown. Take Clark Street the whole way. I'll let you know when we're close.

We head downtown. I look out the window. Diversey, Fullerton, Armitage, North Avenue slide by. I've never been in a limo before, never kicked back and smoked cigarettes, drank beers, had the window down, sat in a car full of a breeze off the lake, the good one, the one before the alewives and the heat turn it into a grey-green fog of summer stink that gets in your clothes and your hair and your heart and makes you long for winter and its clean, cold blast of white scour, and you know just how lucky you are. Never.

Vassily. Hang a right up here when you get to Kinzie. Take it all the way across the river.

River?

Yeah. The Chicago River.

Fuck. This crazy talk. Since when Chicago have river?

Have you ever been down this way before?

Sure. Vassily making joke. Been here plenty time.

You lie, Vassily. I drag out the dipthongs in the first two words.

Well, are certain people, perhaps, "unfriendly" to poor Vassily. Not like Vassily at all. And Vassily hear talk about place call "Shelter" down this way. On Fulton. Map here say just past Kinzie. This place have many bad men hang around. Men Kiev, not Crimea. Many asshole. Too close for Vassily comfort.

Don't worry, man. A few blocks away in the city can be like a whole nother country. You'll be fine.

Okay, boss man. Whatever you say.

Damn straight, I think to myself. *Whatever* the fuck I say.

We pull up in front of the China Club about ten minutes later. Vassily seems relatively calm, but Ziggy doesn't appear to be too amped for this part of the night. He's sitting in the back of the limo doing lines and frantic finger exercises and seeping into the pleather. Tells me he'll just hang out while I go inside and take care of business, whatever the fuck that means.

I say, Don't tell me, man. There's some super-pale gangster-type dude hangs out in the China Club, looking to take you out for your ill-considered choice of hair color.

Heyyyyy, what, man? It's not like that. I'm just tired.

Tired?! I laugh. Fuck, man. You look like you're about to blow a head gasket. You can't be serious. Tell me something else. At least don't insult me.

Okay, jeeeez. I just . . . hate this kind of scene, man, this kind of music.

What the fuck, man? We manage all kinds of bands, bunches of musicians, you need to . . .

Excuse me, boss man. Vassily wondering do any of your so-called famous bands have playing of *trembita* or even *kobza*, because if answering no, then Vassily maybe making deal for you . . .

Vassily. Dude. Don't interrupt me with your bullshit music to blow goats by. Jeeezuschrist, man. I'm trying to talk this guy out of a cardiac episode and you're pitching me some Uki band that scores peasant porn flicks between albums. Give me a minute, would ya?

Is just suggestion . . .

Dude.

Okay. Vassily sorry.

Goddamn. How the hell am I supposed to run this circus? I lean over and do one of the big fat lines Ziggy has cut and chug another beer. Back to Ziggy's bullshit about not going inside.

Dude. Let's go.

Heyyy. No. You go. Have a good time, he says.

You know what? Fuck it. You assholes. Fine. Hook me up with some shit, then. You can't expect me to go in there without a couple of bumps, at least.

Ziggy makes quick with a dollar bill folded up with about a third of a gram inside and hands it to me.

Fine, I say again. But if I come out here and you two are monkey fucking, or elephant walking, or there's any other weird shit going on, you're both fired, and I'm driving the car back up north.

Vassily rubs at his cheek and glances at Ziggy in his rearview. He makes a meh face and rolls up the divider. Ziggy looks for all the world like that guy in that great story, the one where old boy wanted to be a tattoo artist and since his buddy worked in a mortuary he let him practice on the corpses and it was fine except for the one time he tattooed "X"s over the closed eyes of one of them, hahaha, pretty funny tattoo with the irony and all except the guy was a vampire and he woke up and he was a little pissed. Yeah. Like that. I feel generous for some ungodly moment and tell Zig not to worry about it. Ziggy visibly relaxes (such as he can) and I think what the fuck and get ready to go inside.

I roll into the China Club, arms wide open (lol Creed), looking for a crew, hahaha, jokes, but I'm at least expecting a rowdy good time. Hmmm. This sucks. Even though I'm a little wasted, I find myself completely off base—this place is drier than a popcorn fart. There's a gaggle of lechery old dudes clutching martini glasses and checking out the waitstaff hustling trays between what look like private rooms, and I'm thinking this can't be right, but thankfully, I suppose, after navigating some labyrinthine corridors, I start to sniff out too-sweet perfume, bro-sweat, frustrated pheromones, and watery top-shelf drinks. Here be douchery.

My city-kid instincts are on point. What the fuck. It looks like Hieronymus Bosch painted a frat exploding in the middle of a financial district career fair that has an '80s hangover. Greed-is-good-style white-collared blue oxford shirts and yellow power ties assault my twin senses of taste and decency. Judd St. Elmos and Molly Ringfires are everywhere, guffawing with their big nostrils and tittering behind their weird, pale hands, the kind that you see in early Renaissance paintings where they don't look quite right and you find yourself counting the fingers, trying to moor them in some kind of reality you've never known yourself. That line about stealing bread and decadents floats out of some hidden speakers, and I ask myself who would do that, and I answer my own question, saying, St. Just, motherfucker, that's who, and I think, Man, him and *La Montagne* would take out this entire neighborhood, let alone club. I smile big and make eye contact with a bartender I've seen around, maybe at Metro or something, and he gives me the almost-imperceptible head nod and the quickest of eye rolls, like only good bartenders can. I return the greeting the exact same way and look around for smallish dragons and dogs with human asses for heads.

Seeing none, I dejectedly make my way to the bar. My fellow guild member shakes my hand, asks me what I'll have.

I'd really appreciate a Rolling Rock and a double shot of Jäger.

Here you go, cuz.

Thanks, man. I didn't know you worked here, too.

Just filling in during this conference thing, he says.

Ah. Got it. Good money? I ask, throwing back the shot.

Yeah. The tips suck, though. What the fuck?

These are all new rich young assholes, or wannabes, I say, and set the short rocks glass down on the bar. I go on, They all work at the Merc, or the Board of Trade, and hardly ever tip, unless they're trying to impress some chick. You need to work for the wealthy, homes. Those people are normal and know about gratuities.

Maybe next time, he says. You want another pop, or something for the road? I gotta get back to the other end of the bar.

Better give me two more cold ones of these, man, if you don't mind, I say, downing the beer and throwing a twenty up on the bar. Bartenders don't pay for drinks. We tip.

Coming right up, man, he says, and plops down two of the six beers I know he'd been keeping on ice in the well for himself.

Appreciate it. Hey. Do you know where the conference bands and shit are at in this place?

Yeah. Cut through those doors at the back of the bar . . .

Where Andrew McCarts is trying to fuck Demi under her sweaty-ass polyester business suit, or over where Estevez is doing lines right on the table?

Over by Emilio there.

Got it. Have a good night, cuz.

You, too, brother.

I make my way past Kevin and Jules trying to fuck like a pair of eighty-year-olds drunk on sloe gin fizzes who don't know how to get their adult diapers off and end up making angry face at each other instead while they do lots of nostril breathing. I slap both of them on the ass and tell her it's going to be okay, that Kevin'll make enough money for her divorce settlement to buy her a real man, and then head on through the double doors I'm hoping will lead me to some salvation. Another minute of Aramis or Drakkar Noir and coked-up jackassery by sack-tapping frat bros and their jersey-dressed sorority sisters who never put out on the first date but will blow you in the bathroom at lunch on the second might just kill me dead. The sons and daughters of super-pale WASPS with big banana chiclet teeth, who smile like super-happy horses marveling at their own success even in the face of subpar dental work and mediocre intellect are not to be messed with, or mixed with. I think, though, that sometimes when the classes do mingle on occasion, you can get the very best of low-key conflict available; situations that result in free personal ads in the back of the *Reader* like this one:

> CBOT Trader—
> If you say your trampy clerk's name in your sleep one more time, I will pour boiling water onto your balls and then into your open, screaming mouth.
> > Sincerely,
> > Your Wife

I blast through another set of doors and damn. The shit is going on. Mostly real people are hanging out, drinking, having fun. Talking shit, laughing, doing lines. Sure, there's some douchey hey-baby dudes hanging out, but they're getting no play. Chicks are rolling their eyes at them and puffing air out their lips and blowing their hair up off their smooth and unconcerned foreheads. Youth and booze and drugs hum around the room, and the future is so secure no one even gives it a second thought. We smile and sweat at each other, sex or getting high or just ooohing and aaah-ing at our own good fortune is all we want in this moment.

Since I'm on a roll, I stop and think, I'm glad Ziggy isn't here, but it would be okay I guess to have that silly Vassily fucker in here with me. I'm not sure why that is, and then I imagine how great it would be to have him go back in that other room and help me kick the shit out of a couple of those dicks from the Board of Trade. And then I think, Fuck that. If I want to do that, I'll do it myself, all Lit-tle Red Hen style.

I hang out for a bit, getting a little drunker, hitting the bath-room, doing bumps, giving what's ups to various people I vaguely know, and thinking, Man, I've got to get going. I look around and down the bar; nothing going on there. I look out across the club, and I see there's a little stage area way on the other side of the floor. I start to head over and

Ah

Push it

What?

Ah

Push it

Holy crap.

Oooh, baby, baby

Baby, baby

Dang.

Alright, shit, holy man. I get to the little stage and yuuuuup.

It's them.

I drink a little, hang back, check out the show. Way too many white guys here. And girls. No one's dancing, moving, doing any-thing.

I get up closer. Watch the show. They. Are. Killing it.

DJ Spinderella is going to town. I chug my beer. Set the empty down on someone's table. Pull out the seal. Do a blast off the anatomical snuffbox. Light a smoke. Check it out.

Then,

I just can't take it.

I stroll up front-center stage. I'm feeling the cut. I get the look. I'm dying.

I'm getting checked out.

I get the come here finger wave.

No way.

And

high as a motherfucking Afghani fighting kite, I dance my ass off with Salt *and* the Deadly Pepa.

Where's Griffith Park again?

THUNDERBIRD

I finally light this cigarette that's been hanging out of my mouth while I've been digging for some matches. After I take the first drag it rips a piece of skin off my bottom lip because I left it there too long and it got stuck. As I take to cussing and trying to stop all the blood, I accidentally step on this baby bird that must've fallen out of its nest . . . I hear its little dry bones splinter. I make a face.

Muck was an asshole. And that's not that big a deal—assholes can get shut down. But his buddy Jimmy? Jimmy was a prick. Not the kind that just farts in an elevator, but the kind that hits the stop button and *then* cuts one. And then laughs. Because, okay, if you're downtown in a big law building or something and it's early in the morning it kind of already smells like farts and cologne so what's one more, and—ha—these jags have to spill their coffee and huff it up, so yeah, funny. Also, there was this other Jimmy who didn't say much, and he was pretty cool.

Muck, the two Jimmys, and this other motherfucker whose name I can never remember decided that Friday was the best day to kill someone. That it was Friday, sure, maybe I get that, and the weather, probably. You know those summer days. The ones when those warmest of southern winds pick up, say things to you you don't want to hear but can't wait to hear, all in the smallest, thinnest wedge of the day—that time when in between the rain that's coming and the floating in your chest feeling under your hands as you walk, the wind and leaves fly up damp and dry all in the same gust, the breath you leave the same breath you take that one moment holds all summer there for you and only you.

It's that breath but kind of like the breath too of a bar that exhales out into the milk-eye ash-colored street the heat of the summer night, door open at the bar sweating, listening to the radio, the beer warm but still cooler than the thick, thick air, the air that carries the drone of flies out to the haze of arc light where now there are tables and chairs and yuppies but really it was like a stoop and a bucket back then and you can still smell the cigarettes and the old warm beer, shit, they don't make any more like Schlitz and Stroh's and Special Export and, man, this is the greatest, you're just *just* drunkbuzzed, and life

never

gets

better than that, does it?

Here we were on this perfectest of days, and these assholes want to kill Tiger. (I ask myself, How the fuck is this guy named "Tiger" / "El Tigre," what the fuck, seriously, those are from Asia, right, what's wrong with a jaguar [except short for "jaguar" is . . .] or an ocelot or whatever?) Pretension in gangbanging. I think this is probably right before they sent Gang Intelligence crews after everyone. Those two-man GI units would just beat your ass until they got what they wanted to hear, or tired, or both. Mostly Viet Nam vets and lots of former gangbangers, they knew how to get shit done. And we paid for that. But we learned things, too.

Excellent, I think. But I'm like, No, man. Let's get some more beer.

Nah, they say.

Fuck. It's on. Except one of the Jimmys (and now that I'm saying this I'm remembering that, *shit*, there were actually three Jimmys) drops two hits of acid (wow, you're thinking—*acid?* Yup. You gotta see gangbangers tripping on acid. It *is* like Noé meets Winding Refn, just like you thought it would be.) The other Jimmy snorts some tic and then Muck beats off or something, whatever it was he did to get fired up to humbug. That other guy slow sips his quart of Mickey's Big Mouth and doesn't share. I hide my cigarettes from these fuckers and we all take off for Howard Street, and then we run into Jerry the Brazer.

What's up, Jerry?

'T's up?

Where you going, man?

I gotta go. I just shot Taco Junior.

What?

Yeah. But in the stomach, man. Fuck. I think I can still hear him yelling.

Damnit, Jerry (yeah, haha). We were going to get Tiger.

Fuck. That punk is holding in Taco's guts right now. He's busy. The cops'll be there before you are innyway.

Shit, man.

I say, Told you, jagoffs. Shoulda just kept drinking.

One of the Jimmys, 2 or 3, I'm not sure, makes this face.

I hate when he makes that face, because it means he's thinking. He's not chewing the inside of his cheek like Julius, who does that out of habit but also when he's thinking about punching his girlfriend in the face like he does until one of us says stop, but it's kind of like that face, and I start to thinking this is where it could get dangerous. I can feel this low-key burning in my neck, kinda like tightening up your laces all slow but when you pull and sweat it and yank too hard and you peel back half your fingernail and you think, Damn, that hurts, but it's okay because it reminds you to be more careful, and besides, picking at that drying crescent of fresh nail underneath but not quite pulling it off is a great way to stay awake, and to gamble and remember you're still alive when you forget and you jam your hand into your pocket too fast, digging deep for your keys, or your knife, or whatever it is you keep in there.

Jimmy1 says, Well, fuck it, let's just go. Muck is all fired up to hit Taco Junior and Alejandro (that's Tiger's real name, and the only one I use for him, because ocelots, or whatever), but way too fired up like they get when they know shit ain't gonna happen. I see through that shit right away, but I don't say nothing no way, 'cause Muck is just mean. And I'm not in the mood. I think, Let these fools figure it out on their own; I know what I want to do. I want to drink.

Muck, he says, Now's our chance to get those motherfuckers.

Jimmy2or3 makes that eepy face again, twitches his mouth, and says, You need to listen to Jerry, dumbass. The cops'll be there any minute.

I can't help myself. I want to prolong the agony and stick it to Muck a little bit so I say, Yeah, but it's just fuckin' Taco. You think the cops or even an ambulance are gonna show up for at least a half an hour? We got time.

Jimmy1 says, Man, fuck that shit. I'm not getting popped for that. I didn't even get to shoot him. And you know they'll blame my black ass anyway. I ain't goin near there.

Muck looks at us with his head tilted to the side and makes a grimacey face, the one you see where you're like, Is that guy smiling at me or is he thinking about stabbing me or is he trying not to puke, but either way he doesn't look too good. I worry about this guy's blood pressure. A lot. When he gets mouthy, we look at his hair and say to him, Red as the head of a dick on a dog. Man, he hates that. But right now no one's saying nothing.

Time sort of slows down. It gets hotter and even stiller. Everyone looks around at each other like in *The Good, the Bad, and the Ugly*. And in this group we've got some of all three, so this shit is hilarious. Muck grimaces along, frozen in space like a fire-faced gargoyle. Jimmy1 picks at his fingernails and laughs to himself like he does lots of times. Jimmy2 carries on his internal gastric dialogue and kicks rocks into the street. I dream of quarts of Old Style and wonder if that other motherfucker has his .32 with him or not. Fuck.

Since there's no rusty windmills or guys passed out with flies trying to land on their faces and we never know or care what time it is anyway, no clock is going to tick and boom ominously to end this scene.

But the sirens do. And the assholes on the car microphone choose for us, like they usually do.

Hey, you fuckin' punks—stop right there. Teddy! Goddamnit! Don't you fucking move.

Bam. We start running. It's Lenny and Squiggy! Those dipshit cops are actually getting out of the car. Holy. This must be serious. Hahahaha. Off we go behind the Big Pit parking lot and up the side of the railroad tracks. Jerry the Brazer stands there for a minute and then takes off in the other direction toward Howard Bowl and into the smoky poolroom that we can smell from across the street even with the cracked glass doors closed all the way.

The tracks are lifesavers. The Chicago and Northwestern railroad line runs through the middle of the city and takes rich assholes from the North Shore to their grindy, soul-crushing jobs downtown. When we were younger we used to get drunk and moon Chad and Chip commuters on their way home to whatever palaces they live in up that way. The ones where they drink too much, bitch about taxes, ignore their kids, and get buried in golf courses or whatever. Except one of the Jimmys. He would turn around and give them the other kind of windmill. Think about that on your ride home, Biff.

C'mere, Injun! Squiggy yells as he tries to grab me by the hair, and he gets close but not close enough. Fuck that guy. We're running and laughing, big smiley faces washed in light now heading into a new gold sunset that pops up out of nowhere below the low grey cloud line, our eyes squinched against the sudden bright, and we easily outpace the fat, sweaty cops, and I think about the last time we were at Big Pit, local restaurant and home to Howard Street Greasers and junior mobsters in training. Sometimes those guys would help us, and sometimes not, like this one time maybe last summer on a warm, windy night when the moon rose over and over again and

we headed down to Howard Street to fight some Playboys before the truces and alliances were all put together, to the street at the edge of the Jungle (where dime bags good for about eight joints cost ten bucks, hence the "dime" in dime bag—and yeah, that's about seven grams, and we were the only kids in school with a rudimentary understanding of the metric system, which one or two of my teachers liked to point out, but you could get about sixteen pinners out of one and you could sell them for a buck a piece, fatties were two bucks, either way you could make a few bucks AND get high, how cool is that?), home to Howard Street Lords, Latin şãuŋ, and Mexican Playboys. It sucked, because the El stop was there, too, and it was an A/B stop. If you wanted to get off at Jarvis you had to catch an A train or pull the emergency stop, and who has time for that shit?

There's like eleven of us. Skinny shits mostly, except Bubba. You can imagine from the name. We're walking and talking loud and laughing too much, so you can tell we're scared. We're out-numbered in our neighborhood and we know it, but whatever. We go into this fight knowing we're probably gonna get our asses whooped good. We're peewees, and one of the older guys is a junior, I think, maybe, no, it was Giggy from the TJOs, he set up this humbug. I never did find out why. He's not even our set. He says it'll be good for us. I think, Yeah, you know what would be good? You falling down that hole where they're digging up the sewer line on Clark Street and breaking your fucking neck. That would be good, Giggs. On the Nation.

We're walking and Giggs tells us it's going to be skins. No weap-ons. Get rid of those bats and shit. I told them no weapons, he says. I'm like, Cool. I'm good. Except I have my hand jammed in my pocket and around my middle finger are the two rings from the ends of a six-foot dog chain because fuck all that. I'm not even five feet tall right now. Kiss my ass. No way.

We talk tons of shit for blocks, trying to get ourselves worked up for this. The Jimmys and Bubba (no Muck, though, now that I think about it, that fucker), some of the juniors, they want to come check out our skills, and the seniors, well they just sit back and watch it all. I think of some of the shit they've done and seen. Jee-zus. And then I think about it now, now that I'm older, and I still think that. Man.

We're close now. One block over. Birchwood and Ashland. Ash-land is one of the biggest streets in Chicago (Ashland Vikings, Wells High School), but here, this far up on the North Side, Ash-land is nothing. A side street. An afterthought that needed a name. Like a lot of us.

We keep walking. It's pure dark out now, and just the yellowy arc lights give up details from the shadows. Giggy goes ahead of us, and then we can see a bunch of gangbangers in the parking lot by the bank. Like us. Wearing baggies. No shirts. Everybody good and browned up. After a couple weeks of Chicago sun, summer, like poverty, makes us all the same color. And it looks like they brought their juniors too, but they're not hanging back. They all want to humbug together. What the fuck, Giggs? we say. And those motherfuckers have bats and shit. I see a chain slowly swinging, winking under the arc lights, and tighten the grip in my pocket. The other guys look around. Shit, man. Folks is nervous. I say, Damn. This is gonna be hard. Mo-ther-fuck-er. I keep my glasses on 'cause shit, whatever. They're already held together with two Band-Aids. Probably going to need new ones after tonight anyway.

Giggy says, Aight! They're gonna drop their sticks and shit, and then it's on. You fuckers ready!? We say, Yeah, bitch. Get out the fucking way if you ain't helpin', and Giggy says, Y'all bout to get a whuppin' but hold up the flag, brothers! On the love! All the Playboys start yelling, talking shit, hey pinche puto! and fuck you, Royals! and it's getting louder, and I smile a little like whatthefuck and . . . shit. I'm about to head in and get it over with, I'm jazzed, I'm sweatin', I'm seeing silver everything and red tinges the edges and

this car skids up

under the streetlight

and I look at it and through it and I see the Huck Finn donuts that my dad would bring home like twice a year (bestfuckingdonutseveryoubetyourass)

and this car is a burnt-orange or maroon Lincoln, or a Newport, like a 1962 or so, and

oh shit.

A double-barrel shotgun comes out of the back window . . .

Fuck.

I know who this is.

And rips a hole in the night, blasts twice

while one kid falls by the wall by the bank, I

remember him, can see his hair that would've grown out by the time school started again, but then it was still black and fuzzy, tiny-spiked, still close to his skull, and I could see the light hit in between the smallest spots on his head, his skin brown and oily like mine, and then all the little lights went out and he hits the ground and it's

Taco Senior, Big Taco, that fucker

Corona

King

Murderer

and shit, we all laugh, crazy like 'cause holy fuck,

and we take off back up Birchwood, running like some scrawny-ass motherfucking devils with their hair on fire, and I can't help it, I say, Get 'em, Giggs, you fuckin' bitch puto hillbilly, and I think, Man, if he lives he is going to beat my ass, but thems the breaks, init, hahahaha, I laugh. And we go and we cross Clark Street and run into Big Pit. Big Frank says, Get the fuck outta here, and we start to back out, but some of the Grease, they say, What's up, boys? and we say, Big Taco, and they're like, Here, cut through here, and we head to the back and the door just past and they give Frank the look and then I hear someone say, Donny, grab that 12-gauge, and then I remember why we always gripped to the HSG and why most of their set was in jail.

They hook us up with the quick escape proper and we hit the tracks running. I rip my leg open on this rusty piece-of-shit fence I didn't see in the dark, but my brain tells me save it for later letsgoletsgoletsgo. We run for a few blocks and finally stop. We look behind us, and nothing. No one. Just the tracks and heavy-with-summer trees rustling in the dark.

The moon is up. I'm warlord, so I do a quick headcount. Yeah.

We're all here. Bubba's fixin' to pass out though. I'm like, Brother-man, calisthenics should be your best friend. Fuck you, Teddy, he says, and we all laugh like it's the funniest thing ever and it kinda is because I look around and everybody's in one piece and holy shit. Anyone hurt? I say. Nah, they all go, by parts. I'm good. All good. Cool. *Frrrrrrrippppp*, Jimmy goes. I say, Did you just shit your pants? Hahahahaha, we all crack up. Dang, they say in the blue-blue light. Let's get the fuck out of here. Let's go to Farwell. I'm tired of concrete for tonight so I say, Man, let's get some beers and hang out on the tracks . . .

And then I'm walking back to work, back to my own soul-crushing job, and all around me are red-walled canyons of brick and warm air blowing up from the street every time a train passes in a tunnel below, and there in front of me is a herd of fuckin' pigeons, and I think, Goddamn, I hate these fucking things (and remember how one of the Jimmys would feed them from a bench in the Lincoln Park Zoo where we used to go when I could talk the boys into a day of watching the wolves and the buffalo—What the fuck, Teddy?! they'd say. Let's go check out the gorillas. And I'd say, Man, if I wanted to watch a monkey beat off we could've just hung out at your house and saved the dough—and then that Jimmy would throw his coat over the flock and jump up and down on the closest one, and I was like, Jeezuschrist, Jimmy, get a grip, but then he always had dough and would pop for French fries and shit so whatever), and I guess the proper term here is "flock," not something cool like "kettle of nighthawks" (which we had all over the neighborhood) but the actual word you think of when you think of a shitload of birds, yup, this flock of pigeons takes off in front of me like they do, and they're fiddlyfuck flying around, and then there's this . . . shadow, but not really a shadow, more like a greyed-out knife-edge of pressure I can feel above my head, and then *bam* there's like a shock wave and this *ploomph* sound and a crack of hollow bones that comes from the center of the birdspray, and then just some feathers float down and all the other pigeons flap away in rolly-eyed terror, and I watch this falcon streak home supper to her young about fifty-five stories up, and I just keep looking, looking.

SOME AFTERWORDS

Little Thunder Girl

They say once there was a little girl, a daughter of the Thunders. She was playing one day, and looked down, and saw all the little ones playing below. She felt lonely and decided that she wanted to play with them. The Thunders said no, but she begged and pleaded, and finally they gave in.

She came down and they all played together, running, jumping, making up games, all the things children do. But then the little ones had to go home, and so they left. Little Thunder Girl was alone, and lost. She went every which way she could, but all she could see were trees and hills and places that she didn't know. The Thunders called out to her, and the sky turned dark with their anger when she didn't cry back. She called out to them, but they couldn't see her, couldn't find her, and she cried and slumped to the forest floor, not knowing what to do.

After a while, after the winds and the sky calmed down, a swarm of yellow butterflies appeared. They went to Little Thunder Girl and showed her where to find food, where to sleep, and how to be safe. They did this for forty-two days, and Little Thunder Girl was happy and safe with the help of the yellow butterflies until she was able to find her way back to her family, to the Thunders.

For the missing, and the missed, and for my brother Chris Brooks, who gave me this story and said I should tell it.

Acknowledgments

Last summer we came into town, and right at Big Bat's when my phone got service I got an email saying the press was interested in my book. This year, same time, same place, they told me they would be putting it out earlier than we thought.

Well, now. I got work to do.
Here
we
go.

Chicago.

It took me a long, long time to figure out what you meant to me, why I have your flag tattooed on me, and the map of your streets and Els and subways like my veins and arteries and pictures from across the neighborhoods playing on the screen in my head. And then in my forties I went, Hey, you're my rez. I love you and all of us, your folks, so fiercely, so completely, I think about you every day.

Amie, for telling me to write these stories. Emily and Max, for listening and reading.

For Jim and Diana Gehring, who provided the love of my life, my wife Amie, as well as the space where I put together my first book, which was a collection of someone else's work but gave me the courage to think I could do one of my own. Also, some of this intro stuff written in the middle of a very cool lake in Kentucky. Thank you.

Mark Turcotte and Gordon Henry for getting me to write these damn things in the first place. That snowstorm in North Carolina, all two or two and a half inches of it that grounded me in a hotel in Charlotte for three days after a NALS one time, where I started to put this all together. So of course then all those Clan Mothers and Brothers. Especially Gwen Westerman and LeAnne Howe. Jill Doerfler. My brother from another mother, Niigaan Sinclair.

The good Dr. Jones, Stephen Graham. Man. You rock. Thanks for the reads, the bleeds, the seeds that dot these alleyways and blacktops and big western roads and spaces. You let us know we can do this work and make us do it better. Ten thousand thank yous. And those will still never be enough.

NALS folks for listening to and even promoting this . . . whatever you've got in your hands right now. Steve Sexton. Billy Stratton. Royce Freeman. Shaawano Uran and Carol Warrior. Denise Cummings, Scott Andrews, Brian J. Twenter, Susan Bernardin, Joanna Hearne, Brian Burkhart, Padraig Kirwan, David Stirrup, and David Carlson. Mr. Carl Davidson. Brendan Hokowhitu. Dr. Jace Weaver—I did this instead of the other for the moment. I'll get caught up. *Transmotion*, James Mackay.

Vine Deloria Jr. My first inspiration, my greatest book thefts, my orientation to the world when I needed one so badly.

Dennis and Russell, for getting me through all that . . . America. No one but you two and John could've done it, could've centered me the way you did. AIM.

To my fucked-up childhood—yay! But also crystal radio kits and boomboxes—On the AM dial, Super CFL and WLS, on the FM—hey WDHF/WMET. The Loop. ZRD. WLUW and even XRT sometimes. BMX 103 and WVON/GCI 105.9 For Lovers Only and Saturday Night House. All the good stuff. WVVX for a minute— sorry, dude, for the time me and Tuite got you to play Venom and you got in trouble, ABC7-TV Friday Night Movies. The Night Stalker, WGN Channel 9 Creature Features and Family Classics and the Bowery Boys and Tonto and Pancho and the Cisco Kid. Even the shitty Cubs games. PBS Channel 11. Channel 32 the Banana Splits and Johnny Quest and the Three Stooges and original Svengoolie and Son of Svengoolie and Channel 44 with the Speed Racer but not Spectraman. That shit was too weird. Every movie theater on the North Side, and the cheap ones downtown. Bruce Lee. Muhammad Ali. And Stephen King, of course. And then I never realized this until I went to buy books for my son one day, but Jim Carroll, and Charles Bukowski. Thanks.

Uptown, land of my birth. I love you. Then, still, and always. #fuckgentrification.

The North ✝ Side. Best side.

The oyate, my tiwahe, tiospaye, Hehaka Oyate, Wakinyan Oyate, Wanagi Oyate, nieces, nephews, brothers, sisters. Stacy Two Lance and Chris Brooks. Elijah, Malia, Mikayla Brooks, ciye

Rick Palmier, my hunka first cousin Ruben and his missus, Summer Pourier, Michelle Weston and Gilbert Jumping Eagle, Mariah Weston, sister / illegitimate daughter Dacia Dauphinais (nice teeth, cool glasses!) and Orren Janis, Ray Briggs, Chee Carroll III and Don Vito, Olman Wilbur Morrison, Jack Conroy, Lisa Brooks, Mike Brooks, Loretta Little Hawk, Latonna Plenty Wolf, Sedona Brings, misun Delane Has No Horse, Unc Paul Forney, Rudy Raymond.

Elise McHugh, editor extraordinaire. You. So wow. Thank you, thank you. All at UNMP.

Tiffany Midge. You know, even though you're a week older than me . . . hahahaha. Your support has meant so much to me, you don't even know. Thank you.

ĐXБꙀꙄ. ☞Cholera Ranch◖. The Rt. Rev. Martin Billheimer. Dig out thy tails coat, my buttling brother. Miss Sally Timms. Hopefully I can come and read some of this in the hometown somewhere.

Speaking of hometown. Bill Hillman, shit, man. Thanks so much. I can't even.

Early readers Sterling HolyWhiteMountain and Smokii Sumac. Hey now.
Mona Susan Power. Thank you. Thank you. Thank you. Thank you.

Ito Romo, for the support and so much for your stories, too.

Adrian C. Louis. The support, that late-night grad school email, your brilliant work.

Sherwin Bitsui, Trevino Brings Plenty, and Santee Frazier for the best first IAIA experience. And for getting a little bit of your poetry in my fiction. Kinda ew, but all kinda good.

All these cool editors and journals and magazines for publishing my pics and stories!
Entropy (x2!—Janice Lee and August Evans, thank you!), *Noted* (Bryn Skibo-Birney, thank you!), *The Raven Chronicles* (thank you Phoebe Bosch and Matt Briggs, and thank you, Phoebe! for the Pushcart nomination), *Yellow Medicine Review* (Tiffany Midge, thank you!), *Literary Orphans* (Mike Joyce and Scott Waldyn, thank you!), *Indian Country Today* (Dina Gilio-Whitaker, thank you!), *Speculative 66* (Leigh Madrid, thank you!), *The Rumpus* (Terese Mailhot, thank you!), *Broadsided Press* (Elizabeth Bradfield, thank you!), *High Desert Journal* (Charles Finn, thank you!), Adrian Jawort at Off the Pass Press; cousin, eff that Sterling, *The Backwaters Press* (Greg Kosmicki, thank you!), *Future Earth Magazine* (Travis Hedge Coke, thank you!).

All the Chicago gangs, including some gone but none forgotten, all the gangbangers named herein and not, then and now and in the future, because we know we're never going away, I wish you all peace. And oh yeah. There's a story for some of you in the afterwords. And maybe if I make a little money I'll buy an $\mathcal{SCR}$ war sweater. Just sayin'.

And finally, during the last revisions (which took place at the Institute of American Indian Arts Low Rez MFA program, where Jon Davis and Ken White [Ken in particular urged me to "Push It"—I hope I did in the right ways] so graciously asked me to give a craft talk and allowed me to present a bit of this book that was generously received by the fine, fine folks there), before sending this off to the press for consideration, James Alan McPherson passed from this world. He was the very first person to encourage my writing. When we met, and talked, oh so long ago, he told me to "write like whatever you're saying is the most important thing being said in the world at that moment." I try to honor that always, and I hope in this work I've done at least a bit of that thing he found so important and made a little elbow room for these stories. Thank you, sir.

As always, the ancestors. We hope we are what you thought we'd be when you did all you did for us, and that we are being good ancestors too.